"You're going to be safe here, Alexandra."

John resisted the urge to reach out and brush away the lines of worry from her brow with the pad of his thumb. He knew what it was like to be afraid. To hurt. To want peace. "I'm going to make sure of it."

"I can't ask that of you. I'm not even sure I should be here. You're not my keeper."

"Someone has to be." John offered her the cookie bowl. "Just think of me and my family as your temporary guardian angels. We'll watch over you."

"A girl can't have too many angels looking out for her." Alexandra bit into an iced cookie and let the sweetness melt on her tongue. She thought of her self-esteem, still tender, and tried to put aside the bad memories. She was strong enough to make a new life. With the Lord watching over her and a few extra guardian angels, she couldn't go wrong.

John's gaze met hers, full of promise, as unyielding as the strongest steel. "You're safe with me. You can count on it."

Books by Jillian Hart

Love Inspired

Heaven Sent #143
His Hometown Girl #180
A Love Worth Waiting For #203
Heaven Knows #212

Harlequin Historicals

Last Chance Bride #404
Cooper's Wife #485
Malcolm's Honor #519
Montana Man #538
Night Hawk's Bride #558
Bluebonnet Bride #586
Montana Legend #624

JILLIAN HART

makes her home in Washington State, where she has lived most of her life. When Jillian is not hard at work on her next story, she loves to read, go to lunch with her friends and spend quiet evenings with her family.

HEAVEN KNOWS

JILLIAN HART

Love Inspired

Published by Steeple Hill Books™

STEEPLE HILL BOOKS

ISBN 0-373-87219-4

HEAVEN KNOWS

Copyright © 2003 by Jill Strickler

Visit us at www.steeplehill.com

Printed in U.S.A.

Dear friends, since God so loved us,
we also ought to love one another.

—1 *John* 4:11

Chapter One

The warmth of the early-spring sun felt like a promise. Alexandra Sims shut the door of her ancient VW, careful of the loose window, and stared at the little town. She could see all of it from where she stood, with shops on one side of the road. On the other, railroad tracks paralleled the town, and beyond, new green fields shimmered.

She'd grown up in a town like this one along the coast of Washington State. So small, her high school graduating class had been thirty-eight. Maybe because of bad memories, she didn't like small towns much. They'd never brought her luck.

But today she felt luck was in the air, and that made her step lighter as she strolled along the cement sidewalk. She'd pulled off the interstate to fill her gas tank and, since she was here, maybe she'd stop to eat lunch and do a little shopping. This was as good of a place as any.

This little town of Manhattan was truly no different from the other small Montana towns she'd passed through since recently she'd thrown what little she needed into her car and fled in the dark of the night.

Few of the buildings were new, many dating from the fifties or earlier when agriculture belonged to the family farmer and not huge corporations. The people who lived here took pride in their town—the streets were clean, the sidewalks swept and not a speck of litter could be found anywhere.

Sparkling store windows tossed her reflection back at her as she halted beneath a blue-striped awning. Corey's Hardware, the sign proclaimed in bright blue paint.

She pushed her sunglasses onto the crown of her head and stepped through the doorway. A bell jangled overhead.

"Hello, there," called a polite male voice the instant her sneakers hit the tile floor. "What can I do for you?"

Whoever belonged to that molasses-rich voice wasn't in sight. Head-high shelves of merchandise blocked the way.

"Where are your ropes?" she called out.

"To your right, all the way against the wall." A handsome athlete of a man came into view behind the long, old-fashioned wooden counter.

She caught a glimpse of dark black hair tumbling over a high intelligent forehead. Brooding hazel eyes, a sharp straight blade of a nose and a strong jaw that looked about as soft as granite. Definitely a remote, unreachable type.

She retreated to the far wall, where everything from braided hemp to thin nylon rope could be found. Lucky thing, because she found exactly what she needed. What she didn't find was something to cut it with.

"How much do you need?" he asked in that voice that could melt chocolate.

"Three yards."

He was at her side, taller than she'd first thought. He was well over six feet, and while he wasn't lean, he wasn't heavily muscled, either. He didn't have much to say, which was fine with her. Really nice and handsome men made her nervous and tongue-tied. Probably because she wasn't used to them—and great guys had always seemed out of her reach.

As gallant as a knight of old, he measured the thin nylon cord for her, giving her an extra foot, before cutting the end neatly and looping it into a tidy coil for her. "Anything else?"

"That should do it."

He was very efficient—she had to give him that.

"I'll ring you up front." All business, he hardly glanced at her as he tucked away the small pocket-knife he'd used to cut the rope. "Let me guess. You're going camping?"

"Something like that," she hedged. "I had a tent disaster last night, so I need to repair the main nylon cord."

"Been there." He led the way down the aisle of kitchen cabinet handles in every size and color, his stride long and powerful. "Figured you for a tourist. This valley's small enough that sooner or later, you meet everyone in it."

She'd grown up in a town like that, but she kept the information to herself. Her past was behind her and she intended to keep it that way. "This part of the country is beautiful."

"Have you been down to Yellowstone?" He was only making polite conversation as he punched buttons on the cash register.

"Not yet."

"The campsites aren't booked up this time of year, so you don't need reservations." He slipped the rope into a small blue plastic bag. "That will be two seventy-one. If you have your tent in your car, you can bring it in and I'll repair it for you. Free of charge. Company policy."

His offer surprised her. She stopped digging

through her purse for exact change to stare at him. A familiar panic clamped around her chest. Patrick was hundreds of miles away and he had no idea where she was, but this is how he'd affected her. Even a store clerk's courtesy frightened her, when there was no reason for it.

The phone rang, and the clerk answered it. "Corey's Hardware. John, here." He spoke in the same friendly voice to whomever was on the other end of the phone.

John, huh? He looked like a John. Dependable, practical, rock solid.

There was no danger here. She had to remember that not every man was like Patrick. She knew it—now, if only her heart would remember it, she'd be fine.

Alexandra relaxed and bent to dig a penny from the bottom of her coin purse.

"Well, now, washers are tricky things, Mrs. Fletcher," John drawled, tucking the receiver against his shoulder. "Maybe I ought to come by this afternoon and put in the right size for you, free of charge, except for the washer, of course. That'd be the best way to get the job done right."

See what a nice man this John was? He helped all sorts of people. There was no reason at all to feel uneasy. She watched as he swept her coins into his palm as he listened to Mrs. Fletcher.

Nodding, he dropped the money into the cash register till. "Sure thing. I'll give you a call before long."

He tore off the receipt and slipped it into the bag. "I appreciate your business," he told her. "Bring in your tent if you want."

"Thanks." She could do it herself. She zipped her purse closed and reached for the little blue plastic sack. The last thing she wanted to do was to rely on anyone else ever again. She'd learned that lesson the hard way.

A note pinned to the back wall behind the counter caught her attention. Help Wanted. Full-Time Position.

The rest of the printing was too small to read as she swept past. A full-time position, right there, posted for her to see. She'd been praying for just this sort of an opportunity.

Maybe she should ask about it. Surely it wouldn't hurt.

She took a look around at the neat shelving, the tidy merchandise and the polished old wood floor. This wasn't what she had in mind. She'd been a cashier long ago, and she wouldn't mind being one again, but working alongside a man—no, no matter how nice he seemed. Not after what she'd been through.

"Do you need anything else?" John asked from behind the counter, polite, clearly a good salesman.

"No, thanks." She grabbed the doorknob, the bell jangled overhead and she tumbled onto the sidewalk. A cool push of wind breezed along her bare arms.

The advertisement troubled her. Was it coincidence that she'd spotted it, or more?

Unsure, Alexandra unlocked her car door, stowed the rope on the back floor behind the driver's seat and grabbed her hand-knit cardigan from the back. The soft wool comforted her as it always did. Pocketing her keys, she continued down the cracked sidewalk toward the grocery at the end of the block.

The store bustled with activity as weekend shoppers chatted in the aisles and in the checkout lines at the front. Feeling like a visitor in a foreign land, Alexandra headed to the dairy section. The refrigeration cases were the old-fashioned kind, heavy glass doors with handles, reminding her of the small-town store where she used to shop as a girl.

This was not the kind of place where she wanted to live, she told herself as she selected a small brick of sharp cheddar that was marked as the weekly special. She'd left small-town life forever three days after graduating from high school and had never looked back.

Then again, living in a bigger city hadn't exactly worked out well, either.

She wove around two women who looked to be about her age, chatting in the aisle, with their toddlers belted into brimming grocery carts, and felt a pang deep in her chest. What would it be like to live those women's lives? Alexandra found a bag of day-old rolls that still felt as soft as fresh.

The Help Wanted sign in the hardware store kept troubling her. It was frightening not knowing what was ahead of her. Worse, not knowing if she would be able to build a new life. She had to trust that if the job at the hardware store was what God wanted for her, then He would find a way to tell her for certain.

"Why don't you go ahead of me?" A woman with a small girl in tow gave Alexandra a smile. "I have a full cart, and you have only a few things."

"Are you sure?" When the woman merely nodded, Alexandra thanked her and stepped in line.

She'd almost forgotten what small towns were like—the friendliness that thrived in them. A coziness that felt just out of her reach—as if she could never be a part of it. But she enjoyed listening to the checker ask an elderly woman about her new grandbaby.

Everyone seemed to know everything about a person in a small town, she reflected as she placed her cheese and rolls on the conveyer belt.

Why, if she actually were to interview for the job and got it, she'd be easy to locate. If she stayed here, she would probably be known as the new woman in town, even ten years from now.

No, if she took a job anywhere, it had to be in a larger city where she could blend in unnoticed and be harder to track down.

"Did you find everything all right?" the checker asked.

"Yes."

"That will be three eighty-three, please."

Alexandra pulled the fold of bills from her jeans pocket and peeled off four singles.

"Are you enjoying our countryside?"

"It's very beautiful."

"This time of year we don't see too many tourists and Yellowstone is about ready to open some of its entrances, but I think it's the best time to sightsee."

Alexandra hardly knew what to say as the checker pressed change into her palm. "Have a good day."

Even the bagger was friendly as she handed Alexandra a small paper sack.

Taking her purchases, she headed for the electronic doors. Everywhere she looked, she saw people chatting, friends greeting one another, and heard snatches of cheerful conversations.

After the stress and noise of living in a city, she liked breathing in the fresh-scented air. It was so quiet, the anxiety that seemed to weigh her down lifted a little and she took a deep breath. Longing filled her as she headed back to her car. A yearning for the kind of life she'd never known.

Fishing the keys from her pocket, she watched the woman from the checkout line lead the way to a minivan parked in the lot. How content she looked, carrying her small daughter on her hip, opening the back for the box boy who pushed her cart full of groceries. Full of dinners to be made. No doubt she'd drive to a tidy little house not far from here, greet her husband when he came home from work and never know what loneliness was.

That life seemed impossible to Alexandra. Wishful thinking, that's what it was. Maybe, someday—if the good Lord were willing—she'd have a life like that, too.

In the meantime, she had a lot troubling her. She grabbed her water bottle from the front seat and tucked it under her arm. Clouds were moving in overhead, but the sun still shone as brightly as ever. The weather would hold for a lunchtime picnic.

When she spied a little ice-cream stand through the alley, she headed toward it. At the far end of the gravel parking lot, there was a patch of mown grass shaded by old, reaching maples.

Perfect. There were picnic tables beneath the trees, worse for the wear, but functional and swept clean. No one was around, so she chose the most private one. The wood was rough against her arms as she spread out her rolls and cheese.

A car halted at the ice-cream stand's window. As the driver ordered, she heard the murmur of pleasant voices like friends greeting one another.

Alone, Alexandra bowed her head in prayer and gave thanks for her many blessings.

John Corey knew the look of someone hurting. Maybe because he knew something about that. For whatever reason, he couldn't get the woman out of his mind as the minute hand slowly crept up the face of the twenty-year-old clock his uncle had hung on that wall decades before.

She was beautiful, no doubt about that. Not in a flamboyant, look-at-me sort of way, but pretty in a quiet, down-deep sort of way. And those wounded-doe eyes of hers made him wonder what had become of her. She hadn't been back to let him repair her tent, and that disappointed him.

Only because he wanted to do what he could, that was all. Helping was sort of his calling. Sure, he owned a hardware store in a little town that was so small, a person could blink twice and miss the entire downtown. But being part of a community meant being aware of its needs.

He'd gotten in the habit of helping out where he could, fixing eighty-year-old Mrs. Fletcher's outside faucet, for instance, because a widow on a set budget might not be able to afford a plumber.

He'd also come to believe that the Lord gave everyone a job in this world. And that his job was doing what he could. Like the beautiful young woman—there he went again, thinking about her. She'd looked as if she had the weight of the world on her slim shoulders, and, in a way, it was like looking at a reflection of himself.

Some might say her problems weren't any of his business, and they might have a point. But what if she did need help? What if there was something he could do? Lord knew he had a debt to pay this world, and he'd seen her look at the Help Wanted sign he'd posted behind the counter. Did she need a job? But before he could ask her, she'd bolted through the door and was gone with a jangle of the overhead bell and a click of the knob.

And now that it was long past the noon hour and not one customer had been by the entire hour, he had plenty of time to think on what might have been. Plenty of time to notice the little yellow Volkswagen was still parked outside his front window.

Not any of his business, he reminded himself as

he finished his microwaved cup of beef-flavored noodles at the front counter. She didn't want help repairing her tent. Fine. Still, something nagged at him, troubling his conscience.

You're just thinking of another woman you couldn't help. John couldn't deny it, and it left him feeling as if he had to do something, no matter how small, to help even the balance of things.

He was crumpling the noodle container and tossing it into the garbage bin in the back when it came to him. Working quickly, he dug his way through the messy storage room until he found the small kits he'd received a few months ago.

With one of them tucked under his arm, he hurried to the front. Just in time, too. He spotted her through the display window, unlocking her car. Her long dark hair tumbled around her face, a face more beautiful than he'd seen in a long while. Wearing faded jeans and a fuzzy white sweater, she caught his attention and held it.

Like a good Christian man, he ought to be concentrating on his good deed. But what did he notice? Her slim waist and her lean, graceful arms. She'd settled behind the wheel by the time he made it outside and since she'd rolled down her passenger side window, he did what any good man would do.

He leaned on the door and peered through the window. "Need any help, ma'am?"

She squinted at him as she settled her pink plastic sunglasses on her nose. *"Ma'am?"*

"I'm trying to show off the manners my mama raised me with."

That made her smile, and it was a sight to behold. Dimples teased into the creases bracketing her mouth as she flipped a lock of molasses curls behind her shoulder.

What was with him? He had no business trying to make a pretty woman smile. No right to notice her beauty.

He cleared his throat, hoping to sound more gruff. "I've got something for you. Call it a visitor's gift for every new customer through my door."

"I don't need a gift."

"It's a tent repair kit." He handed her the package through the window. "It's got everything you need. Since you've already experienced one tent disaster, you could have another. It never hurts to be prepared."

"It certainly doesn't." She stared at the kit he offered, her soft mouth turning down in a frown. "How much does this cost?"

"Not a thing."

"I'd hate to be indebted to you."

"What debt? I didn't mention any debt."

"Nobody does something for nothing. It's a hard fact of life."

"The kit was a free sample to me from the manufacturer, trying to get me to order a whole batch from them. My storage closet is full of them. You'd be doing me a favor by taking one off my hands."

How wary she looked. "All right. Thank you."

"No problem," he replied, already backing away. "You take care now."

That was that. He'd done the right thing, he figured. Funny thing was, he couldn't seem to turn around and walk away, or even look away as she bent to set the tent repair kit on the floor, her rich brown hair rioting forward to hide her face. Thick, lustrous curls that made him notice. And keep noticing.

He knew it was the wrong thing to do, but he couldn't drag his attention away from her as she straightened. The amazing fall of hair bounced over her shoulders. He stood with his shoes cemented to the sidewalk as she reached for her keys with long slim fingers.

The hurt—he could see it in her, because it was so like the pain within him.

Maybe that was why he couldn't lift his feet and walk away. Why he watched as she blew her lustrous bangs from her eyes with a puff. She slipped her keys into the ignition, but didn't start the engine.

She leaned across the gearshift instead. "It's odd,

because I have a hole in my tent, too. I decided not to patch because I was trying to make do.''

''On a budget vacation?''

''Let's just say a very tight budget. So tight, I've been praying for no rain, and then you hand me a repair kit out of the blue. It's as if heaven whispered to you.''

''Could be. You just never know.''

''Thank you. I really mean that.'' She started the engine, and blue smoke coughed from the tailpipe.

''How much farther do you think this thing will get?'' he had to ask her, gesturing toward her Volkswagen.

''I know Baby doesn't look like much.'' She snapped her seat belt into place. ''But she hasn't let me down yet.''

''As long as you're sure.''

''Absolutely.''

He watched her head east through town, taking the back way to Bozeman.

He couldn't say why, but it was as if he'd lost something. And that didn't make any sense at all. The jangle of his phone reminded him he had better things to do than to stand in the middle of the sidewalk. He had his own problems to solve, debts to pay.

Redemption to find.

Chapter Two

Alexandra glanced at her dashboard and the temperature gauge. The arrow was definitely starting to nudge toward the big *H*.

Great. A serious breakdown was the last thing she needed. Hadn't she just told the guy from the hardware store that her car was trustworthy? That Baby wouldn't let her down?

It looked as though she'd been wrong. She glanced in her rearview mirror and watched a trail of steam erupt from beneath the hood and rise into the air like fog. Yep, Baby was definitely having a problem. She nosed the car toward the gravel shoulder alongside the narrow two-lane country road.

There wasn't a soul in sight. Now what? She killed the engine and listened to the steam hiss and spit. It looked serious and expensive. Expensive was the one thing she didn't need right now. She hopped out to take a look.

The relief that rushed through her at the sight of the cracked hose couldn't be measured. It was a cheap repair she could do herself, and she was grateful for that.

A cow crowded close to the wire fence on the other side of the ditch and mooed at her.

"Hello, there." Her voice seemed to lift on the restless winds and carry long and wide. A dozen grazing cows in the field swung their big heads to study her.

Great. It was only her and the fields of cows. The green grassy meadows gently rolled for as long as she could see. There was the long ribbon of road behind and ahead of her, but nothing else.

No houses. No businesses. No phones.

It was sort of scary, thinking she was out here all alone, but she'd look on the bright side. If she walked to town and back, she wouldn't have to dig into her remaining funds to pay for a tow truck.

After locking her car up tight, Alexandra grabbed her purse and started out. Dust rose beneath her sneakers as she crunched through the gravel. It reminded her of when she was little, and she'd hike with her younger brothers down the long dirt road to the corner gas station at the edge of town.

Like today, the sun, hidden by clouds, had been cool on her back and the air had tickled her nose with the scents of growing grass and earth. In that little store she'd traded her hard-earned pennies for ice-cream bars and big balls of bubble gum.

Why was she remembering these things? She'd long put that painful time out of her mind. What was coming over her today? It was being here, in this rural place. She'd been careful for so long to live with the bustle of a city around her. Traffic and people and buildings that cast shadows and cut into the sky.

It was a mistake to head east. In retrospect, maybe she should have headed south, through California. A busy interstate would never have brought these memories to light. But in this place, the fresh serenity of the countryside surrounded her. The whir of the wind in her ears and the rustle of it in the grasses. After fifteen minutes of walking, not one car had passed.

The wind kicked, bringing with it the heavy smell of rain. She tipped her head back to stare up at the sky. Dark clouds were sailing overhead, blotting out the friendlier gray ones. After another ten minutes, she could see the sheets of rain falling on the farther meadows, gray curtains that were moving closer. She'd lived in Washington State all her life, so what was a little rain?

The roar of an engine broke through the murmur of the wind. Glancing over her shoulder, Alexandra saw a big red pickup barreling along the two-lane road between the seemingly endless fields.

She prayed it was a friendly truck. That it would pass by and keep going. The closer the vehicle came, the more vast the fields and the sky seemed. The more alone she felt.

Her heart made a little kick in her chest. Come on, truck, just keep on going. No need to slow down.

She didn't glance over her shoulder, continuing to walk along the edge of the ditch.

She could hear the rumble of a powerful engine and the rush of tires on the blacktop. The truck was slowing down.

This wasn't good. Not one bit.

Please, don't let this be trouble, she prayed, eyeing the width of the ditch and wondering just how fast she could get through that fence.

She could hear the truck downshift as the driver slowed down to match her pace. Out of the corner of her eye she saw the polished chrome and the white lettering on the new-looking tires. The passenger window lowered.

Alexandra went cold. Did she expect the worst? Or was it simply that old country code of neighborliness that was at work here?

As if in answer, a little girl leaned out the open

window and tugged off plastic green sunglasses. ''Hi, lady. My dad says I gotta ask if you need a ride.''

At the sight of the blond curls and friendly blue eyes, Alexandra released a breath. She hadn't realized her chest had been so tight.

It just went to show how traumatized she'd been this last year. And that deep down, she expected the worst—of life and of people.

It wasn't something she could brush off lightly. If this past year had taught her anything, it was important to stand on her own two feet. To keep from needing anyone. ''Thanks for the offer, but I don't mind walking.''

''That's what Dad said you'd say, right, Dad?''

''Yep, that's what I predicted,'' answered a molasses-rich voice that sounded very familiar.

On the other side of the little girl, behind the steering wheel, a man tipped his Stetson in her direction. Alexandra recognized that handsome profile and those mile-wide shoulders.

''This has to be more than a coincidence running into you twice in one day.'' John Corey shook his head. ''I can't believe this.''

''Neither can I.'' She blinked and he was still there. The truck's door felt steel-cool beneath her fingertips. ''I thought you had a store to run. What are you doing out here?''

"Since I'm my own boss, I can close up shop for a few minutes. Folks know to wait or give me a call if it's an emergency. Hailey, here, spent the morning out at a friend's place and gave me a call to come pick her up."

"Yep." Hailey swiped wayward curls from her eyes, waving her neon-green sunglasses as she talked. "We had a barbecue picnic and potato salad for lunch. I didn't like the potatoes one bit 'cuz they were the red kind and Stephanie's mom put in those black rings."

"Olives," John informed Alexandra from across the cab. "We're not olive people. We flick them off our pizza if they get on by mistake. The pizza people hear about it, too."

"Rightly so." Not everyone shared her opinion of olives. Okay, so maybe it was all right to let herself like him, just a little. "It's good to meet you, Hailey. I'm Alexandra."

John leaned over the steering wheel to get a better look at her. "Alexandra, huh? I couldn't help noticing your car alongside the road a few miles back. Figured I might come across you on the way to town."

"You seem awfully sure of yourself. How many women fall for your knight-in-shining-armor act, Mr. Corey?"

"Thousands."

"None." Hailey frowned. "My daddy only dates the TV."

"The what?"

"Now don't be revealing all my secrets. A man's relationship with his sports channel is sacred." He flushed a little. "Hailey, open the door for the lady. It's a long walk to town and it's fixing to rain."

"I'm not afraid of a little rain," Alexandra argued, because it had been so long since she'd accepted help from anyone.

Hailey moved back on the seat, as if to make room. "You gotta come with us. It ain't right to let ladies walk."

"You said it better than I could." Leaning past his daughter on the bench seat, John fixed his deep hazel gaze on Alexandra. "Come on aboard. You'll be perfectly safe with us. If you're worried at all, I just want to put your mind at ease. My daughter doesn't bite, and on the off chance she forgets her manners and does, she's vaccinated."

"Daddy." Hailey scowled, scrunching up her freckled nose. "I haven't done that since last year at Sunday school, and Billy Fields bit me first."

"See? We're as trustworthy as can be."

"Trustworthy, huh?"

"Absolutely." John reached over and opened the door.

"We got lots of room," Hailey added.

"You two make it impossible to say no." It wasn't as if she was alone with a stranger. Clearly John had a daughter, so that meant he was married, right? A dependable-father type, so she figured she might as well spare herself the long walk to town.

Something wet smacked against her forehead. The first drop of rain. Drops pelted the road and she dodged them by climbing into the cab.

"Looks like we came along just in time." Keeping his attention on the road, John flicked on the wipers and put the truck in gear. "I told you your car was going to break down. I won't say I told you so."

"You don't have to look happy about it. You *were* right, but it's only a cracked hose. Easily fixed."

"Really? Did you diagnose the problem yourself?"

"Sure. I've been on my own for a long time. I've had to learn to do minor repairs here and there. It's no big deal."

"Let me guess. You're one of those independent types?"

"Something like that."

He continued watching the road and never looked her way once.

Yep, definitely the dependable-father type. There wasn't a thing to worry about. Alexandra relaxed into the leather seat. She'd never been in such a fine vehicle. Warm heat breezed over the toes of her sneakers.

Hailey snuggled close. "Alexandra, do you got a dog?"

"Not anymore. I had a little terrier when I was about your age."

"Cool. Did you love him lots and lots?"

"I sure did. He slept at the foot of my bed every night and watched over me while I slept." Alexandra sighed, softening a little at the rare good memory from her childhood, and secured the seat belt. "I miss him to this day. When I was eleven, we moved to a different house and couldn't take him with us, so I had to leave him with the neighbors."

"I bet that made you real sad."

"It did." Alexandra swiped an unruly lock of brown hair behind her ear, looking down at her scuffed tennis shoes. She couldn't help noticing Hailey's brand-new ones, already scuffed, with bright purple laces. "Why don't you tell me about your dog?"

"Don't got one. Daddy is really mean and won't let me have one." Hailey grinned.

"That *does* sound mean." Alexandra never knew it was so easy to tease.

John's dark gaze warmed with mild amusement as he lifted one thick-knuckled hand from the steering wheel to ruffle his daughter's unruly hair. "Alexandra, don't get the wrong opinion of me. Hailey isn't quite old enough for the responsibility of taking care of a dog. She still can't pick up her room every day."

"Can, too." Hailey's chin jutted out. "I don't got a lotta time. I'm very, very busy."

Alexandra stifled a chuckle. "Busy, huh? I bet a pretty girl like you has a full social calendar."

"Yep. I got swimming lessons and ballet lessons and piano lessons, 'cept I'm not so good at that, but Gramma says I gotta keep practicing my scales, even if I hate 'em."

"Wise woman, my mother." John found his gaze straying from the road again and in Alexandra's direction. "You can see how lonely a dog would be waiting for Hailey to get done with all those lessons."

"I'm not taking your side." She shook her head, scattering those rich brown locks that seemed shot full of light. "No way. I'm sticking firmly with Hailey. A girl needs a dog of her own. It's one of those rules of life."

"Like death and taxes?"

"Exactly. I'm so glad you understand."

"Daddy didn't have a dog when he was little." Hailey leaned close to whisper. "Don't ya think that means he's *gotta* have one now?"

"Makes perfect sense to me," she whispered back.

"You're getting me in trouble, Alexandra." John guided the big pickup around a curve in the road. "Have pity for a poor beleaguered dad."

"Yeah, you look like you have it tough." She didn't feel an ounce of pity for him—only admiration. For the obviously comfortable and good family life he had. His daughter didn't sit quietly, afraid to make too much noise. No, Hailey wasn't afraid to sparkle. The affection between father and daughter was clear.

No, John didn't have it tough. From where Alexandra sat, she figured he had everything important in life.

Everything she'd never had.

"Hey, enough about us." John cut into her thoughts. "Tell us where you're headed once you get your car fixed."

Alexandra tensed. It was a perfectly innocent question. She knew that. John didn't mean any harm. She knew that, too. He couldn't know he was asking the impossible. She couldn't talk about where she'd been and never where she was going. She had to leave her past behind, and lying was the only way to do it.

The story she'd been rehearsing since that first frightening night on her own was right on the tip of her tongue, but it felt wrong. She couldn't do it. Not to this man and his daughter, who were being so nice to her.

So what did she say? Her stomach clenched as tight as a fist. Simply thinking about where she'd been sent panic lashing through her. She stared at the road ahead, slick with rain. A wind gust roared against the side of the truck and she wished the winds were strong enough to blow away the bad memories she'd left behind, and she was able to find a way to answer him honestly. "I'm not sure where I'm going. I'm just driving."

"You're the adventurous type, is that it?" John slowed the truck as town came into view. "You decide to vacation and go where the road takes you?"

"Exactly." She said nothing more. She was looking for a new life.

And praying she would know it when she found it.

The rain ended and the wind died down as they drove along the main street of town. Modest shops were open for business, and a few cars were parked along the curb, but no one was in sight. Maybe the rain had scared everyone inside.

"Daddy, can we stop for ice cream? Please, please?"

"What do you need ice cream for? You're sweet enough already."

Hailey rolled her eyes. "Gramma says a girl's gotta have chocolate."

"Gramma ought to know. She's a wise woman."

Hailey didn't know what a lucky little girl she was, to have a kind man for a daddy, Alexandra thought as the pickup slowed to turn off the street and into the gravel lot. Then again, maybe like Alexandra's father, this was how John acted in public—polite and deferential.

Home had been a different matter.

She'd learned the hard way it was difficult to really know a person from outward appearances. It was a tough lesson to learn but one she'd never forgotten.

John pulled up to the drive-through window at the same little stand where she'd eaten her lunch in the shade. On friendly terms with everyone, it seemed, he greeted the blond-haired woman by name after she slid open the glass partition.

"Hi there, Misty. We'll have three chocolate cones, double dipped."

Before Alexandra could protest, the woman smiled brightly. "Three it is. I'll be right back." Then she disappeared into the shop.

"Consider it terms of accepting a ride with us," John explained easily. "Where there's Hailey, there's chocolate ice cream. It's best not to fight it. Just accept it as a law of nature."

"Then it should be my treat in exchange for the ride to town." She peeled a five-dollar bill from the stash in her wallet.

"No, it's not my policy to let ladies pay." He held up one hand, gallant as any fine gentleman.

"It's my policy to pay back good deeds when I can." She pressed the bill on the dash in front of John and gave him an I-mean-business look.

"This goes against my grain," he told her, handing the five to Misty at the window in exchange for three huge chocolate-encased cones. "Thanks. Hailey, pass one down."

"These are awesome." The girl's eyes shone with pleasure as she handed the biggest cone to Alexandra. "You gotta be careful 'cuz the ice cream is all melty."

"I see." The rich chocolate smell was enough to die for. Her mouth watered as John put the truck in gear and circled around to the shaded picnic tables.

Random raindrops plopped onto the windshield from the trees reaching overhead. "This looks like a good place to have a car picnic," John announced. "What do you say, Hailey?"

"A truck picnic, Daddy," she corrected with a roll of her eyes. "My Grammy loves car picnics. Don't you, Alexandra?"

"A car picnic, huh?" She'd never heard it called that before, but it wasn't hard to see at all, sitting in this comfy truck with the heat breezing over their toes as father and daughter picnicked right here, out of the weather. It was way too much for her and far too tempting to stay.

A gust of breeze buffeted the side of the truck, reminding her that she was like the wind. On the move, with no place to call home and no reason to linger.

There was nothing else to do but to tuck her purse strap firmly on her shoulder. "You two enjoy your picnic. This is where I go my own way."

"No! Wait," Hailey protested. "You gotta eat your ice cream."

"I will, I promise." Alexandra popped open the door and her feet hit the rain-sodden ground. "I hope you get your puppy. John, thanks for the ride."

"Wait." He bolted out the door. "You don't have to run off. You're going to need a ride back to your car."

"I don't think your wife will appreciate your driving strange women all over town." Alexandra took a step back, putting safe distance between them. "Don't you have a job at the hardware store to get back to?"

"I own the store, and my part-time hired help can handle things while I'm chauffeuring Hailey around." The wind tousled his dark hair, drawing her attention to the look of him, and the way his shoulders looked as dependable as granite. "I'm not married. Not anymore."

"My mommy died when I was just a baby," Hailey added around a mouthful of ice cream.

"I'm sorry." The words felt small against the size of their loss. Somehow knowing John was a single father made it easier for her to take another step away and another, her heart feeling as heavy as stone.

"It's a long walk back," John called after her.

"I don't mind." She waved goodbye across the gravel lot and disappeared before he could say anything else.

Crunching the last bite of his cone, John had to admit the chocolate didn't taste as good as usual. That was Alexandra's fault.

When he'd happened along her broken-down car on the road, he had to wonder if he was meant to help her out. A woman alone like that... Surely the Lord was watching out for her. Surely it had been no coincidence John had been the one to find her walking toward town. The good Lord knew John had debts to pay and never turned down an opportunity to do so.

It troubled him now. He tried to put thoughts of Alexandra aside as Hailey told him all about her morning at Stephanie's, but his mind kept drifting back. God hadn't intended for people to be alone. That's what families were for, neighborhoods, churches and towns.

He couldn't help wondering if Alexandra was about ready to walk alone back to her car.

The clouds overhead had broken, but the real storm hadn't hit yet. He could feel it in the wind and smell it in the air.

"Let's get going, Hailey. We can't leave Warren in charge of the store for much longer." The high school kid he'd hired was reliable, but he was young. "Look at you, all covered with chocolate."

"I made a real mess," she agreed cheerfully as she rubbed her hands on a wadded napkin. "Is Grammy gonna come pick me up now? 'Cuz I've got lots of stuff to do."

That was his daughter, always on the go. "Yep. All I have to do is give her a jingle. Turn your head that way. You really smeared yourself up good this time." John grabbed the last paper napkin and wiped the chocolate smudges from his daughter's face.

"It was really melty. Hey, Daddy?"

"What?" He gathered the trash and tossed it into the garbage bin. "This isn't about getting a dog again? You're wearin' out my ears on that one."

"Oh, I don't want a dog. I want a puppy." She

climbed into the cab and plopped onto the seat. "A *puppy*."

"That's just a little dog."

"Yeah, but you let me have a horse."

He got into the truck, turned the key and listened to the engine rumble. "That's it. I forbid you ever to visit Stephanie again."

He gave her head a ruffle, and she giggled, light and sweet—his most favorite sound of all.

Back at the store, Warren was helping a customer, so John grabbed the phone and dialed. He counted nine rings—Mom must be outside in her garden.

She was out of breath when she answered. "Hello?"

"Hailey's ready for you."

"Oh, John, perfect timing. I was starting to wonder about her. Say, grab a container of rose food for me. I just ran out."

"Will do. And since I never charge you a penny—"

"Uh-oh, I'm in trouble now. I can hear it coming." On the other side of the phone, his mom had to be smiling. "All right, I'm sitting down. What do you want now? Don't tell me you finally folded on the puppy issue."

"Not yet. I'm still waging that battle. Listen, on your way to town, you'll see a woman walking.

She's medium height and slim with dark brown hair and wearing a sweater and jeans. Give her a ride back to her car, will you? Don't take no for an answer.''

"I should hope not! A woman walking alone. This country is safe, I'm proud to say, we're a fine community, but a woman shouldn't be left alone. And walking on that long road. Why, I'll leave right now.''

"You're a good woman, Mom.''

"Don't I know it.''

John punched the button, ending the conversation. Problem solved. Alexandra wouldn't be able to refuse his mother. Few people could. Alexandra would get the help she needed, and his conscience could finally stop troubling him.

End of story, he told himself, heading back to the garden section. The phone rang and more business walked through the door, enough to keep him busy. So, why couldn't he stop thinking about Alexandra and the way her smile never quite reached her eyes?

Chapter Three

"I just can't leave you here." Bev Corey set her jaw, sounding as formidable as a federated wrestler instead of the tiny slip of a woman standing alongside the country road. "What if your car doesn't start? Dear, I truly believe we should call a mechanic."

Alexandra couldn't help liking the woman. Bev Corey may be a stranger, but in the ten-minute trip from town, she almost felt like a friend. "Don't worry. I've done this before. I'll show you."

"That's what men are for—to keep cars running smoothly. And it's my belief that's what we should let them do. My Gerald is a hop and a skip up the road. Let me go hunt him down, and I'm sure he'll be happy to fix this for you."

"Thanks, but I can handle it. All I have to do is replace this hose, and I'll be on my way."

"That simply seems dangerous." Bev took a tentative step forward, as if to keep far from the grease. "Engines explode, metal parts can burn you. There's acid in the battery, you know. I don't think it's safe for you to be touching that."

"The engine is cool and I'm far away from the battery." Alexandra tugged the damaged hose loose. "Now I just fit this on here—"

"I'm not sure about this at all. Why, those are out-of-state plates. How far have you driven this poor car? I don't know a thing about engines, but this certainly looks as if it needs a mechanic's attention." Bev shook her head, scattering the short, perfectly coiffed curls, which slipped back into place. "What were your parents thinking, to let you take off across country in a car like this?"

It seemed natural that Bev should ask, obviously being a motherly type. Still, it hurt to look back. Remembering couldn't change the past or the family she'd been a part of. "I left home when I was seventeen and I've never went back."

"Never?"

"No. I'm happier that way." If it still made her sad, she tried not to feel it. She'd been fine all these years on her own, with the Lord's help, and even though she'd had a rough time lately, that was all about to change. She was sure of it.

She changed the subject as she wrestled the hose into place. "Have you always lived here in Montana?"

"Goodness, yes. My family homesteaded the land in the 1880s. Five generations of Coreys have farmed that land. We grow potatoes and are proud of it. Montana is a fine place to live. Are you thinking about moving here?"

"It's a possibility," she admitted before she realized she'd spoken.

"Are you here looking for work?"

"I'm looking for the right opportunity." Alexandra slammed the hood and tugged on it to make sure it was latched.

"So you've come to interview for a job?" Bev lit up. "Why, that's wonderful. So many of our young people are moving away to the bigger cities. Are you interviewing right here in our town?"

"I don't have an interview, not yet," she corrected, wiping her hands on the edge of a rag. "I'm looking and hoping the right job comes along."

"Trust in the Lord to see to it, dear. What kind of work do you do?"

"I clean houses."

"Honest work. And hard work."

Alexandra pulled her key from her pocket.

"Thanks again for the ride. I'm glad I got to know you."

"Don't say your goodbyes yet. We'll wait and see if that car of yours starts." Bev looked doubtful as she eyed the rusty Volkswagen.

Alexandra unlocked the door, settled behind the wheel and turned the ignition. The engine didn't roll over, so she pumped the gas—but not too much so she wouldn't flood the carburetor.

She got out and once again moved to check the engine.

"Just as I thought." Bev planted both hands on her hips, leaving her fine leather purse to dangle at her side. "That car isn't drivable. Do you realize what a godsend it was that John gave me a call?"

"John called you? But I thought you were on your way to town—"

"And so I was. But John asked me to keep an eye out for you on my way in and give you a ride back to your car. He's my oldest son. Always with a hand out to help, that's our John. Land sakes, what are you doing now?"

"Cleaning off the battery terminals." Alexandra bent over the engine compartment. "That's probably why my car isn't starting."

It took only a few seconds to wipe the terminals down and tighten the connectors.

"Something tells me you've been on your own a

long time.'' Bev eased closer. ''No boyfriend? No husband?''

''No husband. Yet.'' But there had been a man who'd proposed to her after three years of dating. A man she'd been ready to marry.

Panic clawed in her chest and she said nothing more about Patrick. She wanted to forget him, to forget she'd ever known him. She slammed the hood and took a deep breath. ''This should do it.''

''If it doesn't start,'' Bev warned, apparently expecting the worst, ''then you'd best come with me and no arguments. I can't in good conscience leave you here.''

''She'll start.'' Alexandra gave her car a pat on the dash and turned the ignition. The engine rolled over, coughing and sputtering, but that was normal. ''See? I know she doesn't look like much, but she really is a reliable car.''

''I don't know about that!'' Bev didn't look convinced. ''It's Saturday afternoon, and it's sure to be dark soon. What if this car of yours breaks down again?''

''Then I'll fix it. The great part about having a car this old and uncomplicated is that I can fix nearly everything that can go wrong with it.'' She liked Bev, and wished her own mother could have been more like the woman standing before her now. ''I'll be fine, so don't worry. You've helped me more than you know.''

''I feel as if I haven't done a thing. Maybe you should come home with me tonight. I've got a little rental cottage out behind the garage. It's as tidy as could be.''

Alexandra bit her lip, not at all sure what to think. She'd been too long living in a city and had forgotten what it was like to live in a small town. Forgotten that in small towns, the world seemed kinder. It was hard to trust in that kindness—in the belief of that kindness.

Her chest ached, as if a part of the defensive wall around her heart crumbled a little. She'd learned long ago that kindness hurt, too, because sometimes it hid pity. ''Thanks for the offer, but I want to reach Bozeman by nightfall. Once I'm there, I'll see where my path takes me.''

''But you're alone. How old can you be? Twenty?''

''I'm twenty-four.''

''Why, my youngest daughter is that age. I'd hate to think of her alone, driving across country in an unreliable car.'' Bev opened her leather purse, which exactly matched her shoes. ''Let me see…where is it? Here, my husband's business card. You promise to give me a call tonight, when you get settled.''

"Sure." Alexandra took the card and ran her thumb across the embossed letters.

Gerald Corey, Potatoes And Soybeans, it said, and listed an address and phone number. There were different logos, probably farmer organizations she didn't know anything about, but she did know one thing. Bev was genuine in her caring.

It had been a long time since someone had truly cared about her. A long, lonely time.

Bev was a stranger, and she probably treated everyone she met this way. With warmth and concern. As if they were family.

"I'll call when I'm settled," Alexandra promised, tucking the business card into her back pocket.

As she settled behind the wheel, she couldn't help feeling hopeful. That this short stop in this little town was a sign of things to come. Good things the Lord had in store for her.

It was hard to say goodbye, but she managed it. Harder still to put the little car in gear and ease onto the road. Waving, she shifted into Second, watching Bev grow smaller in the rearview mirror.

Alexandra felt as if she were leaving something of great value behind, and she didn't know why. Bev Corey climbed into her luxury sedan, and then the road turned, taking Alexandra around a new corner and down a new path.

It made no sense, but the feeling remained.

* * *

''Here's Grammy,'' Hailey announced from the front of the store. ''See ya later, Dad!''

''Don't forget your bag.'' John watched to make sure she grabbed the pink backpack from the counter, damp from the towel and swimsuit inside from her stay at Stephanie's. ''And wait up. I've got something for your grandmother.''

The bell above the door jangled and the screen door slammed. Hailey hadn't heard him. Through the front-window display, he could plainly see his mom circling around the front of her car, dressed perfectly as always, and greeting Hailey with a big hug.

His pulse skipped a beat—then he noticed the passenger seat was empty. Mom hadn't brought Alexandra back with her. Disappointment washed through him like a cold ocean wave, leaving him troubled.

Had he been looking forward that much to seeing Alexandra again?

Then maybe it was for the best that she wasn't here. He had no right to feel any caring—however remote—for any woman. Not after how he'd failed.

Through the screen door, he heard his mother talking, and his daughter answering. He could hear a hay truck downshift as it eased through town. It all sounded far away at the memory of his failure long ago now, but yet, in an instant, it seemed like only moments ago. When his world had changed. And a pretty young woman had lost her life.

The container felt heavy in his hand. Praying for the memories to leave him, he pushed blindly through the door, stumbling and dazed. He'd do anything to have the chance to go back and change the past. *Anything.*

Mom's merry voice brought warmth to the afternoon suddenly turned cold. "Hailey, that bag of yours is as wet as your swimsuit. We'd better put it in my trunk because I just cleaned my car. Is that everything?"

"Yep." Hailey took tight hold of Bev's hand, as she always did, and climbed into the back seat.

A typical Saturday afternoon, like a dozen others so far this spring. Mom's cheer, Hailey's charm and his life in this small town—the same as ever. The weight of his guilt made his step heavy and slow.

"John, are you all right? You're as quiet as could be, and that's not like you." Mom peered at him carefully. "You don't seem flushed."

"I'm fine. Just wondering if you found Alexandra," he hedged.

Why was his pulse racing when he mentioned the woman's name? It was guilt—plain and simple. As if he could help enough people, that would atone for the one person he couldn't have helped.

"Heavens to Betsy, John, I'm so glad you called me. I found poor Alexandra walking along that road all by herself. That just isn't safe, not at all." A deep look of sorrow passed over Mom's gentle face. She'd always been tenderhearted, caring about everybody.

"I insisted on giving her a ride, and you were right, she was stubborn at first, but that shows sense. A young woman can't accept rides from strangers these days. So I stayed with her until her car started. But do you know she doesn't have a soul in the world who cares about her? No family at all. No one to worry over her arriving safe and sound. It's a shame, it is, a nice girl like that."

"That's why I called you." John's throat tightened until he could hardly speak. "Thanks for helping her out."

"She bought us ice cream," Hailey volunteered from the back seat. "And she had a dog when she was little. Just thought I otta mention it."

"We heard you, Miss One Track Mind." Bev tried to hide a chuckle. "We'll pray Alexandra has smooth roads ahead of her. You were a good man to help her out, John."

"The least I could do, seeing as she came into my store."

"You don't fool me with your modesty act.

You're one of the finest men I know, and I'm proud to call you my son.''

Not true, but it made some of the pain in his chest ease. ''I come from good stock,'' he told her because he knew it would make her smile, and he turned to his sprite of a daughter playing with the seat belt buckle. ''You stay out of trouble, you hear?''

''I'll try.'' Hailey grinned like the angel she was.

Such sweetness. Love for her filled his heart as he set the bin of rose food in the trunk with Hailey's backpack. She was a good girl, and he was grateful to his mom for the time she spent with Hailey, making up for a mother's absence.

His guilt felt as dark as the storm clouds overhead.

''Bye, Daddy!''

John watched his mother's car pull away from the curb. Hailey's purple-painted fingernails flashed as she waved.

The Lord had forgiven him long ago, or so Pastor Bill assured him time and time again, but that hadn't erased the guilt. John would never forgive himself for his wife's death.

Ever.

Because he'd stopped by Mrs. Fletcher's house, John was late arriving at his Mom's. The kitchen was a flurry of activity. The oven timer buzzed loud and shrill, and the potatoes boiling too hard on the stove spit sizzling water onto the burner.

"Good, you showed up just in time." Mom poured water from the green beans at the sink. "Give your dad a shout, would you? He's out tinkering with that tractor and I can't get him away from it."

"Daddy!" Hailey looked up from coloring at the table. Crayons flew as she tore across the room, winding her arms around his knees. "Grammy's making my favorite potatoes."

"Good. Those are my favorite, too."

The phone shrilled again just as Mom was reaching deep into the oven to rescue the delicious-smelling roast. Halfway to the door to find his dad, John lifted the receiver from the wall-mounted phone. "Howdy."

"Is this Bev's home?"

Wait. He knew that voice—soft, pretty and gentle. "It surely is. This wouldn't happen to be Alexandra?"

"Hi, John."

"How's the car running? Mom told me you were quite the mechanic."

"I managed to make it to Bozeman just fine. I promised Bev I'd call when I arrived safely. So she wouldn't worry."

"That's my mom. I knew she'd look after you."

"I should hold that against you, sending me someone I couldn't say no to. Thank you."

"You're more than welcome. Here's Mom now. Before I surrender the phone—" he held the receiver high so his mother couldn't reach it "—I meant to say something earlier, and since this is probably my last chance, here goes. I noticed you taking a second glance at the Help Wanted sign I had posted. You wouldn't happen to be interested in a job, would you?"

"I'm surprised you noticed. I hardly glanced at it."

"So you aren't interested."

"I didn't say that."

On the other side of the line, Alexandra could hear Bev telling John something.

John chuckled. "Is that so? Mom said you were looking for a job. For the right opportunity."

"How do I know working in your store is the right opportunity? I have absolutely no hardware experience whatsoever."

"You don't need experience. I'm not looking for help in the store."

"You're not?" Her heart gave a little jump. "You mean you need someone like a bookkeeper?"

"Nope. I need someone to watch Hailey for me during the week. Mom's only filling in temporarily while I find someone new. The last sitter quit to go to Europe with her family, and how can you blame her for that? But it's left me high and dry. I don't think there's anyone available in all of the Gallatin Valley.''

''But you don't even know me.''

''I know that you like double-dipped ice cream and you're good with kids. That's good enough for me. C'mon—'' Hailey's excited chants filled the background as John laughed. ''See? Everyone's in favor of it.''

The panic returned and Alexandra wasn't sure why. Wait—maybe she did know. The last time she'd been anything more than strangers with a handsome man, it had ended in near disaster.

This was different, she told herself, but the panic remained. Being responsible for a child with all the worries she had about her own safety, that simply wasn't the right thing to do.

''I'd love to, John, but I'm afraid I can't.''

''I appreciate your decision, that you might want to keep your options open in case some better offer comes along. So here's what we can do. Consider it a temporary position and you're free to leave for a better opportunity. What do you think now?''

''I think you're trying to make it impossible for me to say no.''

''True,'' he admitted, warm and deep, like richly

flowing chocolate, and the sound was enough to make her stop breathing and remember how masculine and strong he'd been without seeming cruel or controlling. Just like a hero out of a movie.

Well, men like that weren't real, she told herself, sensibly. They really weren't.

"At least tell me you'll think about it?" he asked.

She held the phone tight to her ear, wishing a part of her didn't long to accept. To spend her days taking care of a nice little girl, baking cookies and playing in the sunshine. She wouldn't be alone—at least for a little while.

And that was almost temptation enough.

"I'm afraid I can't." It was hard to say the words. Harder still to think about hanging up the phone. "I appreciate the job offer, really I do, but I don't think I'm what you're looking for. Goodbye, John."

"Wait! Alexandra—"

She hung up. It was the right thing to do. For John and Hailey. And for her.

"If it's a local call, next time I'll let you use my phone instead of the pay phone," the lady in the office offered as Alexandra swept by.

"Thanks." She smiled at the woman, who then stepped into the back room where she lived with her husband. The aroma of meat loaf lingered.

It was suppertime. Everyone in the campground was settling down to eat. She walked past motor homes, where retired couples chatted over their meals, and tents, where families cooked over open fires. Everywhere she looked, people were gathering in pairs and groups.

One day, that would be her. She was certain of it. Surely the Lord didn't mean for her to always be alone.

Chapter Four

The wonderful thing about camping was that a person never needed an alarm clock. Nature had its own rhythm, one that felt serene and peaceful as Alexandra punched her pillow, nudged awake by the call of birds heralding the coming dawn, and the downshifting of truck traffic on the highway. But Alexandra was content to ignore that as the first rays of the rising sun cut through the nylon tent and into her eyes.

Good thing she was an early riser. Her nose was cold from the chill in the air, and for one second she snuggled deeper into her toasty-warm sleeping bag. The fabric shivered around her as she turned onto her side. Could she manage a few more minutes of sleep?

But already her mind was racing ahead. It was Sunday—she wanted to find a church service somewhere nearby, and then hit the road when it was over. Would she head east, toward Miles City and North Dakota? Or south toward Yellowstone? The checker at the grocery store had mentioned the park was opening some of its entrances.

Maybe she could find an available campsite, since she'd never had the chance to travel before. This was her first time out of Washington State. Wouldn't it be something to see Old Faithful? Well, she'd simply have to see where the Lord led her on this beautiful spring day.

Already the sun was boldly chasing away the chill from the air. So why lay around like a lazybones? She crawled out of her sleeping bag, deciding she wanted to hit the showers before they got busy. A quick breakfast, and then she'd find a nearby church. The day already felt full of promise.

She crawled out of the sleeping bag, already shivering in her favorite pair of sweats. It didn't take long to grab her bag of showering things and her last clean towel from the stack on the back seat of her car. The campground was quiet this time of morning, except for a few travelers beginning to stir. An older woman, opening her door to the pine-scented air, stepped out of a luxury motor home and offered a pleasant good-morning.

Alexandra returned it, feeling better for the momentary connection. The skies were clear and a dazzling blue. The air smelled fresh and crisp, and she couldn't help feeling full of hope. Surely the happy touch of the sun meant good things for the day ahead. It had been one more night that Patrick hadn't caught up with her.

She showered quickly, shivering in the cold water. Apparently the water heater wasn't working terribly well, but she didn't mind. Cold water was good for the soul, right? She certainly felt invigorated as she toweled dry, pulled on a pair of warm sweats and ran a comb through her hair. Now, to dig out her good clothes from the bottom of the duffel bag, and then she'd go in search of an espresso stand. She was on a budget, but a double hazelnut latte was a once-a-week treat she wasn't about to miss.

With her bag slung over her shoulder, she pushed through the doors and stepped out into the new day, where the sun was up, so warm and bright it hurt her eyes to look into it. Surely there was an espresso stand close by, and if she could find a local paper, then she could check the church listings—

"Alexandra!"

She froze in the middle of the dirt path. She didn't know anyone here. For a nanosecond, fear speared through her. Then she realized that it was a child's voice that had called her name, not a man's. Not Patrick's.

"Hey! Alexandra. Remember me?" A little girl skipped along the low fingers of light slicing through the pine trees lining the gravel driveway.

Alexandra warmed from head to toe. "Of course I remember you, Hailey. What are you doing here by yourself?"

"Oh, Daddy and Grammy came, too, but I can run the fastest."

John was here? And Bev? What were they doing here? Confused, Alexandra squinted into the long bright rays of the rising sun, but she couldn't see anything. Another flash of panic sliced through her—was she really that easy to track down?

Hailey skidded to a stop, her hair tangled and her purple ruffled dress swirling around her knees. Her neon-green sunglasses were perched on her nose and hid her eyes, but her grin was wide and infectious and adorable.

"How did you find me?" Alexandra tried to keep the panic from her voice. She'd paid cash for one night, and the manager hadn't asked for more than her car's license plate number. That didn't make her easy to track down, right?

"Grammy hit the dial-back thingy. That's how we knew where to come get you." Hailey slipped off her sunglasses. "It's Sunday and you can't *not* go to church. Grammy was real worried 'n stuff, so Daddy said we'd take ya with us. Right, Daddy?''

''That about sums it up,'' answered a deep rumbling voice.

John. Alexandra felt his presence even before she heard the first pad of his footstep. Even before she caught the faint scent of pine-scented aftershave on the sweet morning breeze. The sun rising in the great sky behind him shot long spears of golden light, casting him in shadow as he strode closer. His broad shoulders were set, his Stetson tipped at an uncompromising angle, his gait slow and steady. Confident.

He looked like a hero out of a movie, the tall, dark silent warrior too good to be real. He strolled into the shadows, the change of light transforming him from shadow to flesh-and-blood man. He looked different today in his Sunday best, still rock solid and powerful, but remote. For the moment, unreachable.

Alexandra's breath caught, and she was very aware of her long hair wet from the shower and tousled by the wind. She'd run a comb through it once. Who knew what she looked like? She was wearing her favorite pair of gray sweats, of course, the old ones that were baggy and had holes in both knees.

It doesn't matter, she told herself. It certainly

wasn't as if John Corey was looking at her like a man interested. And shouldn't she be panicking instead of hoping he did like her?

Right. Except she knew there was no danger here. John was a widower with Hands Off practically pasted to his forehead.

"How about it, Alexandra? Seems we owe you for treating us to ice cream, and Coreys always make good on their debts. We can't let this favor you did us go unpaid, so here we are, asking you to ease my conscience and let us take you to church with us."

"It was only ice cream, John. Not a debt to be paid."

"That's a matter of opinion. Come to the service with us. You would make Mom happy. She loves to fuss over everyone. It gets tough on a guy. Think of it this way. You would be doing me a favor."

"Oh? A favor now? I thought you said it was a debt!"

"Semantics." It was easy to see the good in him, the easy charm that he kept rigidly veiled, but it was there, lurking in the friendly grin that would put Robert Redford to shame. "If you came along, then Mom would fuss over you instead of me and Hailey. Believe me, it's a lot to endure, and we need a break. Isn't that right, kid?"

"Yep." Hailey bobbed onto her tiptoes. "Grammy's real mushy. She says it's 'cuz all her kids are all grown-up. And I get too much fussin'. Are you really gonna come, Alexandra? Please? I can show you my horse.''

''Well, I'm not sure—''

Hailey's face fell. ''You don't wanna see my horse?''

Now what did she do? ''Well, sure, but—''

''Don't bother to fight it, Alexandra.'' Amused, John eased closer. ''It's best just to give in. Mom and Hailey together are a powerful force. They scare tornados away. It's best to do what they want.''

''And I don't get any say in this?''

''Nope.''

It would be easier to say yes if he didn't look so strong and dependable. She wasn't sure she liked how she felt when she was around him. She certainly noticed he was a man. The trouble was, she hadn't planned on making connections of any kind. The fewer people who remembered her, the less chance Patrick had of finding her. ''I'll come on one condition.''

John lifted one brow, as if intrigued, leaning a fraction of an inch closer. ''Name it.''

''This settles the score. There's no more debts, no more favors. I don't need any charity.''

''Good, because I'm not giving out any.''

She couldn't imagine a man as polished and probably as financially sound as John Corey would know much about camping. Or about getting by. Nor could he possibly understand how she felt, that she didn't need help the way he thought.

She could stand on her own two feet, on the path God had made for her. And she ought to tell him so, but she didn't. She was tired of feeling so lonely.

For a handful of hours this Sunday morning, she wouldn't be alone. That was blessing enough. A special gift on the Lord's day.

The church parking lot was full by the time Alexandra made it back to the small neighboring town, nestled in the rolling foothills of the Rocky Mountains. The day was dazzling, and the sky endless. The sunshine smiled over her as she squeezed into a space along a tree-lined curb, shaded gently by the first buds of an ancient, sprawling chestnut tree.

"Alexandra!" Hailey dashed across the street, all long limbs and swishing skirts and brilliance. An equally coltish little girl ran at her side, in a white pinafore dress that was every bit as nice as Hailey's high-end department-store jumper. "You made it! You made it! Grammy was afraid you'd get lost."

How wonderful it was to be welcomed! "Me? Get lost? No way. Is this your friend Stephanie? The one with the puppy?"

"That's her!" Hailey bounced to a stop.

"That's me," the girl agreed easily. "You have really pretty hair. Can you do mine like that?"

"Yeah, mine, too?" Hailey begged.

"No problem. It's just a French braid. It's a cinch to do."

"Cool!"

Hailey grabbed one hand and Stephanie grabbed the other, and Alexandra found herself tugged across the street. The two girls began skipping.

"C'mon, Alexandra!" Hailey urged. "We're in a hurry."

"I don't think I can go any faster." Her heels were a little rickety, and her right ankle wobbled. But sandwiched between the kids, she gave it a try.

She hadn't skipped since she was a child. Her feet felt so light. And her hair bobbed up and down with her gait. She felt fantastic, like singing, and she hardly realized she was laughing until she leaped onto the sidewalk with the little girls and skidded to a stop in front of John Corey.

Oh, no. He was squinting at her, and he probably thought that was no way for an adult woman to act, skipping like a child right there in the church parking lot. She was a guest of his, too. She hadn't meant to forget herself like that.

Feeling a little embarrassed, she swiped a lock of escaped hair behind her ear. "Thanks for the escort, girls."

"Guess what, Daddy? Alexandra's gonna make my hair like hers." Hailey bounded over to tug on his hand. "Can Stephanie sit with us? Can she, please?"

"As long as it's fine with her parents." John watched as the girls dashed off, in search of Stephanie's family, skipping hand in hand, leaving them alone.

The wind gusted, cool and strong, and Alexandra shivered. Her feet felt heavy again as she took a step toward the church, where families grouped together in conversation. She was sharply aware of being alone and a stranger. On the outside, just as she'd been as a child.

And as an adult, keeping a firm distance away from men. From John as he swept off his Stetson and raked his fingers through his dark hair. A contemplative gesture as he watched the other families, his face an unreadable mask.

Not that whatever he was thinking was any of her business, but she wondered. Several people shouted out greetings to him as they passed. Apparently John was well woven into the fabric of this community, where everyone knew him by name and reputation, and welcomed him with looks that said John Corey is a good man.

"Alexandra? Ready to head inside? It's got to be

better than standing around here. I feel like I'm in the way.''

''Sure. Hailey told me Bev will be singing in the choir this morning.''

''Yep, she is. We tried to stop her, but she's stubborn. It's a shame, too.'' His dark eyes twinkled with a hint of trouble.

What was it about this man? She hardly knew him, but he could make her laugh. She didn't feel as alone as she kept up with John's long-legged stride, which he kept shortening to accommodate her gait.

She wished she could stop wondering about him. He'd been a widower for a long time. Out of deep love for his lost wife, maybe? That would explain the distance she felt, just beyond his polite friendliness and warm humor. As if he'd closed off a part of himself long ago, barricaded it well and hidden the key.

When the line moved, John motioned for her to take the step ahead of him. He was so close. Too close. The woodsy scent of his aftershave, the faint aroma of fabric softener on his jacket, the faint heat from him made her acutely aware of the six feet of male so close, if she leaned back a fraction of an inch, they would be touching.

That couldn't be good. Alexandra leaned forward

as far as she could, creating distance. Still, the feeling, the sensation of closeness, remained.

"I bet you'll like Pastor Bill." John's warm breath fanned the shell of her ear. "He leans toward meaningful but short sermons. Mercifully short. You can't find that just anywhere."

"Then I guess I'm lucky that you and Hailey hunted me down this morning."

"That's right. Afterward, there's Sunday brunch at my house. You're invited."

She had miles to cover, laundry to do and a future to find. Gazing up at John, seeing the strength and male vitality of him as he towered over her, blocking the sun, every cell within her seemed to take notice.

One thing was for certain—John Corey was not her future. She should say no.

"Come join us. We have plenty to share, and this is the Lord's day. If you don't, my mother will hurt me."

"Sure, like I believe that."

"You should. She's a formidable woman. You should know that by now." He winked in a friendly way. "Just be prepared, that's all I'm trying to tell you. She's going to insist. Personally, I think she's just looking for someone new to impress since we're all tired of complimenting her cooking. She needs you."

"What can I say? I'm in demand. I guess I'd better stay for a little while."

"You've got places to go and people to meet?" he asked, his gaze narrowing, as if he were measuring the truth of her.

"Something like that. I might hop down to Yellowstone. I've never been, and it's only a few hours away."

"You'll be glad you did." He paused while they moved a step closer to the minister. "I've got some old guidebooks for the park. I don't need them anymore, but they have campsites and information. Might come in handy."

"Has anyone ever told you that you are too helpful?" Alexandra twisted around to look at him, the wind tangling the cinnamon-brown wisps framing her pretty, heart-shaped face, making her look vulnerable. Her slim brows arched over her luminous dark eyes in a playful frown. "There has to be something wrong with someone who's *too* nice."

"I toss my dirty socks on the floor just like any man," he quipped, keeping her away from the truth. She had no idea what she'd said, or what her innocent, light comment made resonate deep down in his soul.

The family on the steps ahead of them moved away, saving him from trying to come up with an easy answer, one that wouldn't reveal the pain deep within. His problems weren't anyone else's, and Alexandra looked down enough on her luck that the last thing she needed was to have to listen to his troubles. A wrong he could blame on no one else but himself.

"Pastor Bill." John offered his hand, clasping the older man's warmly. "I'd like you to meet Alexandra."

"What a pleasure." Pastor Bill took Alexandra's slim hand, welcoming and warm. "I hope you enjoy our humble service this morning. We're short a singer in the alto section, if you happen to be willing to join the choir."

"Me? No, but thank you." Alexandra spoke as gently as lark song, her grace unmistakable.

John didn't feel it was good to notice that.

"Daddy!" Hailey called out, as she and Stephanie crowded their way onto the top step.

The girls were laughing, making Alexandra laugh and the minister chuckle fondly. It was a beautiful morning, this day a gift from the Father above, as were the people surrounding him. The girls who tugged on Alexandra's hand, eager to sit next to her in the church, and Hailey calling to him again to get his attention.

He had more blessings than most. More than he deserved.

"Daddy, Alexandra's gonna braid our hair, so we've gotta hurry. There's Grammy in the front! They're gonna start singing. Hurry! Please!"

Hailey's fingers curled around his own, holding on tightly. So very tightly.

Take care of our baby, Bobbie had begged. *Promise me, John. Promise me.*

Pushing down the guilt and a sorrow that had no end, he carefully tucked it away, down in his soul where it belonged.

Steadied, once again back to himself, he managed a smile and squeezed his daughter's hand. Trust glittered in her eyes.

Her hand in his gave him strength as he followed her down the aisle and into the row where Stephanie and Alexandra were already settled.

"Me, first!" Hailey collapsed onto the wooden pew. "Right, Alexandra?"

"Right." She dug through her shoulder bag, bowing her head as she pulled out a comb. Cinnamon-brown wisps, silken and glossy, had escaped from her braid, brushing the soft curve of her cheek.

She's a beautiful woman. The trouble was that he kept noticing that. Over and over again. He found the edge of the bench by feel and dropped onto it. The faint scent of her shampoo—something that smelled like apples and spring—made him dizzy with yearning.

With the wish for a woman to love. Alexandra was so incredibly soft and graceful and everything missing in his life, everything he'd been without for so long. It overwhelmed him. Sharpened the edge of a longing he hadn't felt since Bobbie's death.

The longing for companionship. For the deep, abiding connection of love and intimacy. For that incredibly strange and wonderful way of a woman, of her brightness, of her smile, of her magical softness in his life.

And it was wrong. He squeezed his eyes shut, willing away the longing, just as he'd forced away every other emotion. He tried to focus on the sounds around him—the familiar rise and fall of voices as families settled down into the pews, the strike of heels against the wood floor and the clatter of shoes as the children followed their mothers into the rows.

Hailey's elbow bumped him, bringing him back. He turned toward her, and there was Alexandra. Right there, in his peripheral vision, impossible to miss. She could be an angel, with the colorful light from the stained-glass windows washing over her like grace.

Her slim fingers held and twisted and folded locks of Hailey's sunny-blond hair with deft confidence, fingers that were long and well shaped, feminine and hugged by several silver rings. Nothing fancy or expensive, just artful, and somehow like her.

Her fingernails were short and painted a light pink, hardly noticeable except that he couldn't seem to tear his gaze from the nimble way her hands worked, tucking and folding, and then winding a small lime-green elastic band around the end of a perfect braid.

"Cool! Thanks, Alexandra." Hailey touched her new 'do, shimmering with happiness. "See, Daddy? I think you gotta hire her now 'cuz not even Grammy can do braids like this."

"They aren't hard to do, not at all," Alexandra argued, stepping in as if to save him from having to answer. "Let me grab one of these hymnals. I don't want to be flipping pages when the choir starts."

Hailey jumped to help, and so did Stephanie on Alexandra's other side, as the organ music crescendoed, and Pastor Bill approached the altar.

With Hailey between them, it wasn't as if Alexandra was close to him. But she was. The apple scent of her shampoo seemed to fill the air. He couldn't stop noticing her. The way she crossed her ankles, the left over the right. He saw that her left shoe strap was held together by one of those tiny brass-colored safety pins.

He ought to feel sorry for her, a woman alone, without family, without means, practically living out of her car. That's what he ought to feel. Obligation, duty and a sense of purpose in the chance to help, to right some wrong, since he had so much on his soul to make right.

But what he felt wasn't pity at all. Or charity. Or the sense of accomplishment that came from helping others. He felt…aware of her as a woman. In a way he hadn't taken notice of any woman since he'd met Bobbie. Shame pounded through him, like wind-driven hail, leaving him icy cold and stinging.

Stunned, he rubbed his hand over his face. This isn't good. It isn't right. He had no business feeling anything but duty toward anyone, much less another beautiful woman. He'd messed up his one chance at love, the beautiful blessing of marriage the good Lord had given him. He had no right to even notice another woman's beauty.

The congregation rose with a resounding rustle that echoed throughout the sanctuary. His cue to stand, too. He held the hymnal and tried to follow the hymn he knew so well. But couldn't seem to remember the words because he heard Alexandra's sweet soprano, so quiet it was barely discernible, but to him, he heard only her.

This strange, warm flutter of emotion…it was something he had to control. Tamp down and extinguish, because he didn't deserve it. He didn't deserve her.

Pastor Bill began the prayer. Bowing his head, John pushed away all thoughts of Alexandra and, with all his heart, concentrated on the minister's words.

Chapter Five

Was this the right place? Alexandra pulled into the long curve of gravel driveway that climbed lush rolling fields, and disappeared out of sight. Her tires crunched in the thick, soft gravel as she drove up the incline.

The house swept into view around a slow curve, a two-story log structure with a gray stone chimney rising up into the sky. Smoke puffed from the chimney, and every window facing her sparkled clean and pure with the sun's light. John's house, just as Bev had described it.

At least she was in the right place, although she wanted to turn the car around and speed straight to the freeway. Why? Because she was insane, that's why. She was attracted to John. Attracted—as in liking. As in noticing a man the way a woman noticed a man.

Warning. Danger. Didn't she know better? Remember what happened the last time she felt this way?

She shivered, despite the warm air breezing in through the open window. Trembled all the way down to her soul. If she closed her eyes and looked inside herself, she knew the memories of Patrick would be right there, close to the surface, frightening as he grew angrier and more threatening, his fist raised....

Don't think about it. She took a deep breath and gave the door a push. Warm, grass-scented air caressed her face as she climbed out of the car. The gravel crunched beneath her heels and the wind tousled her skirt hem.

Maybe it was the day, or the way Pastor Bill's sermon had lifted her heart, but she felt as if the world had never looked so beautiful. The sky was a dazzling blue—truer than any blue sky she'd ever seen before. The mountains jagged and snow-capped, awash with sunlight like a row of uncut amethysts, enduring and breathtaking. Like faith.

Good things were in store for her. She simply had to believe.

"Alexandra! Come meet Bandit!" a cheerful voice called out, drawing Alexandra's attention to the shadowed side of the garage, where Hailey perched on top of a chin-high wooden fence. She was no longer in her Sunday best, but in a pair of jeans, boots and a grape T-shirt. "Do ya like horses?"

"I'm sure I'll like yours." John wasn't in sight, so Alexandra gladly headed straight down the cemented path that hugged the long wall of the garage. Lilacs lifted budding lavender cones, brushing her arm and skirt as she swept by.

She still didn't see John. He was probably in the house. Good thing. Considering how she'd been feeling this morning, aware of his presence, of his warm breath on her ear, it was best to avoid him as much as possible. He was obviously a nice guy, but she didn't feel comfortable being alone with any man.

"My horse is named Bandit and I can ride her really good," Hailey called out, swinging her feet. "See how pretty she is?"

Alexandra hardly glanced at the horse. What she noticed were two very big, very male boots visible beneath the horse's belly.

John straightened up, knuckling back his hat to study her over the saddle horn.

She skidded to a stop, her dress swirling around her. She felt melty inside, the way Hailey had described her ice-cream cone the other day. Melty and aware and uplifted. Just from seeing John.

Not good. It was best to ignore it. "You have a beautiful horse, Hailey."

"I know. Bandit's my very, very best friend, next to Stephanie and Christa. Oh, and Brittany, but only sometimes." Hailey flipped her bouncy ponytail behind her shoulders. "Do ya wanna ride? I'll let ya, if you want. I only let my best friends ride Bandit."

"I'd be honored, except I don't know the first thing to do with a horse."

John strolled out from behind the mare, moving with the slow power of molten steel. "You can learn. It's easy enough."

"Gee, thanks. I was hoping it would be really hard. I'm afraid of heights."

"Then I won't torture you. I'll just take you mountain climbing instead." Laughter flashed in his dark eyes. "Hey, I'm glad you found us okay."

John hardly glanced at her. He doesn't feel this same zing of interest that I do, she thought. Why was she disappointed?

John's attention was on his daughter, as it should be. Capable and gentle, he swept the little girl from the high rail of the fence to the soft grass-strewn ground beside the horse. "Want a hand up?"

"Nope, I can do it. I'm big and stuff." Hailey jabbed her toe into the stirrup, reaching high for the saddle horn. She stretched to her limit and struggled to mount up. John stood behind her, ready to catch her if she should fall.

Just like a good father should.

Her heart tumbled in her chest—a sign of doom. Don't start seeing a fantasy where none exists, she reminded herself. That's the mistake she'd made with Patrick. She'd seen all the wonderful things he was, and ignored the not-so-wonderful.

Big mistake. One she wouldn't make again.

"Hey, Daddy! It's Grammy!" High atop her horse, Hailey pointed toward the driveway, already sending her mare into a run. "Gotta go, okay? Bye!"

They were alone. Just the two of them. She pretended to watch Hailey ride off, waving to her grandmother. But she was really trying *not* to notice John.

It was impossible.

Alexandra felt his presence, as if all her senses were honed onto him and nothing else. The sound his boot made when he placed his foot on the bottom fence rung. The whisper of his shirt sliding against the rough wood as he settled his forearms on the rail. The fall of his shadow across her feet.

"I'd better go see if Bev needs any help." It was the only excuse she could think of, but it gave her reason to leave.

Except she felt the unmistakable weight of his gaze on her back, watching her walk away.

Watching her. That didn't sound good. But when she glanced over her shoulder, John was lifting a sun-browned hand to his mother.

Not to her. Heat fired across Alexandra's face. See? More proof that he isn't interested. This reaction to him was probably exhaustion. She was putting in long days on the road. She wasn't sleeping that well at night. She was off-kilter and so were her feelings. Right?

Trying to make herself believe that explanation, she hurried through the shadows and into the blazing sunlight, leaving John behind.

Bev was unloading plastic containers from the back seat of her luxury sedan. "Oh, there you are. I'm so glad you decided to join us. I made my special potato salad, which I usually only make for special occasions, but I was in the mood for it yesterday. Now I know the reason why."

Bev handed over the large container she held, reverently, as if it were priceless. "Heaven above must have known we'd have you for Sunday dinner. Hailey, go tell your father I hope he remembered to get propane for the barbecue."

"But, Gram, I really, *really* need a cookie. I'm gonna starve or something." Hailey leaned over the top rail, while her horse stood placidly. *"Please?"*

"We can't have you keeling over from starvation, now, can we?" Pretending to be stern, although her eyes were twinkling merrily from behind her bifocals, Bev popped the top of a Tupperware container and held the bowl over the fence. "Just one, and it had better not spoil your appetite, young lady."

"I'm as hungry as a horse." Hailey bit the corner off a bright pink iced cookie. "I'll go tell Daddy."

"That's my girl."

Alexandra helped herself to a few of the containers on the back seat. Might as well be useful. See how easy it would be not to think about John?

"Providence has sent you to us, I have no doubt of that." Bev gathered the last two bowls, tucking both of them neatly into the crook of her arm. "I want you to take a look at John's house. You'll see right off how much he needs to hire someone, and fast."

"Ah, now I know why you invited me to Sunday dinner."

"I confess to ulterior motives. But it just seems too perfect, is all. Hailey and you get along pretty well."

"I think she's a great kid."

"See? I knew I liked you."

"I have great taste when it comes to people." Alexandra didn't know how else to say it. "Thanks for inviting me today, Bev."

"My pleasure."

Alexandra's heart felt incredibly light. She'd needed this more than she'd realized. She'd been so unhappy with Patrick, and slowly growing unhappier with every day that passed, that she hadn't noticed how bad it was.

And how much of life she was missing out on.

"See?" Bev pushed wide the ornate front door to John's house and held an arm wide to the living room. "What can I say? Disaster. I've been trying to do what I can, of course, but what he really needs is a wife."

"He's looking to remarry?"

"Oh, I hope and pray. No, Bobbie's death broke his heart clean in two, I tell you. I keep hoping he'll find love again. Then again, who knows when it comes to the heart?"

Alexandra's throat tightened, and she couldn't speak. She felt sad for John and his wife, and surprised at Bev's words. Love like that didn't exist, did it?

"What happened to her?"

"A climbing accident. Something went terribly wrong. John blames himself. He cherished her, you know. She was his everything, and he hasn't been the same since he buried her." Sadness etched into Bev's face, deep around her eyes and mouth, a measure of her own grief and loss.

Real loss. It washed over Alexandra like a tidal wave. Cold and powerful, she was left reeling as Bev tapped away through the foyer and along chinked log walls where framed pictures were the only decoration.

Pictures of family. Of Hailey smiling on top of her pony, her cowboy hat lopsided, grinning while she held a melting grape Popsicle. Pictures of Hailey as a toddler, so small and laughing, cradled in John's protective arms. Images of Hailey as a downy-haired infant tucked beneath a pretty woman's chin— John's wife.

It was impossible not to feel sorry for him. John's heart was broken irrevocably, Bev had said. Did people really love one another like that? Or was it the fondness of the memory, the sorrow of loss that made the past seem better than it was? She didn't know.

"I'm ready to start grilling." John strolled through open French doors and into the impressive kitchen. "Mom, you're making Alexandra work, and she's our guest of honor."

"Oh, I don't mind—"

He stole the bowl from her arms, standing so close to her that she could smell the comfortable scents of barbecue smoke and mesquite chips clinging to the sweatshirt he wore. Standing this close, she could see into his eyes. How dark they were, instead of filled with light. From grief?

Alexandra remembered the picture of his wife, and how gentle her smile had been. She didn't know what to say as John stepped away and snapped off the plastic lid of the container.

"Mom, you are a wonderful woman. I was hoping you would make this." He inhaled deep. "I'd better sample this. Just to make sure it's good enough for everyone else to eat. I'm a pretty good taste tester. I'm going to get me a spoon—"

"Stop that." Bev playfully slapped the back of his hand as he pulled out a cherry-wood drawer in the center island. "I know what you're up to, and you'll wait to eat like everyone else. Really, John. You'd think you were a boy again. How is that going to look to Alexandra, when she's trying to decide if she wants to work here or not?"

Uh-oh. Alexandra stepped forward. As gently as she could, she tried to say, "Bev, I'm not—"

"You are?" John interrupted, turning with the bowl in the crook of his arm. "Great. I'm glad you're reconsidering. Look at the mess I'm in. Wait. Don't look. It might scare you."

"I wish I could, but I can't—"

"Just give us a chance, dear." Bev snapped open one container after another. "You could go other places and work for other people, but who could need you more than us?''

''You're pulling my leg. This place is immaculate.'' Alexandra's throat tightened, looking around at the cozy, well-appointed home.

''Hailey needs you.'' John scavenged through a drawer for a spatula. ''If that makes a difference.''

Alexandra didn't know what to say. She'd been looking for a new start. The chance for a new life.

Could it be true? Is this what the Lord had in His plans for her?

''What do you think?'' John squinted across the outdoor table at her, shaded by a big yellow umbrella, as she took her first bite.

''Heaven with mayonnaise.'' Alexandra couldn't help a tiny moan of appreciation.

''See, Mom? I told you.'' John reached for the serving spoon. ''Since it's been officially tested and approved, I'm done waiting. I'm digging in.''

''Serve your mother first.'' Bev winked, holding out her plate, fully aware she was torturing her grown son. ''Two big spoonfuls, please. How about you, Hailey?''

''Yep. I want lots.'' She held out her plate, too.

''In some houses, it's the man who gets served first.'' Good-natured, John winked, and dumped a heaping serving of potato salad on Bev's plate.

"In some houses, in the fifth century. Don't forget to serve your father. Gerald, only one scoop. We're watching his cholesterol." Bev leaned close to confess. "Alexandra, go ahead and start passing the chicken. Take a nice big piece. You'll love John's marinade. Hailey, honey, pass the biscuits, please."

John and his father were talking about a tractor engine, their voices pleasant rumbles as Alexandra selected a piece of deliciously fragrant chicken and set it on her plate. There was no strained silence, as she'd grown up with. Or the pretense of rigidly polite manners that had been so important to Patrick.

Hailey was chattering away to her grandmother about her horse, and Bev was filling both their plates with wonderful food. Sweetly spicy baked beans and a green salad and biscuits so fluffy they looked like miniature clouds. Ice tinkled in a crystal pitcher as John refilled his glass with iced tea.

"You're pretty quiet." He reached the short distance between them to fill her glass, too. "We're an overwhelming bunch, aren't we? My brother and his wife will be coming along after a while—they're split between two families on Sunday. They usually bring dessert. Then it will really get wild. Ice cream. Cake. Scandalous."

"You do this every Sunday?"

"Pretty much. Sometimes we meet at Mom and Dad's. Sometimes here. Depends on who's in the mood to do the most cooking.'' John dropped spoonful after spoonful of sugar into the tall glass. ''I want you to know my offer stands. The job is temporary if you want it that way. Sort of a test run, if you want. I pay well.''

''I'm sure you do.'' Now she felt uncomfortable. How could she admit why she couldn't take the job? She started to tremble, a quivery feeling that raced from her midsection down to her toes. ''This isn't what I'm looking for.''

''Then what is?''

How could she tell him what she was really afraid of? ''I have my reasons.''

''I suppose it's because of my mom. You heard her sing in the choir and the noise she makes scares you.''

''Nope. I think Bev has a lovely singing voice.''

Bev preened. ''Thank you, dear.''

John stirred his tea, making the ice cubes tinkle. ''You won't stay because of Hailey. She's a wild one with all those lessons. You're afraid you'll run yourself ragged ferrying her to and from. She has a busy social calendar, too.''

''I have piano lessons tomorrow,'' Hailey announced. ''Alexandra could take me 'n stuff.''

''Fine, make it impossible to say no.'' Alexandra knew how to play this game, too. She met John's gaze without batting an eye. ''The real reason I'm not sure I can take this job is you, John. I heard you sing in church. I absolutely cannot work for someone who's that tone-deaf.''

''She's got your number, son!'' Gerald called out.

The family broke into howling laughter.

Wouldn't it be wonderful to stay here? The delicious salad tasted dry on her tongue as she tried to laugh along with Bev's gentle teasing, and John's good-natured banter in return.

Her heart became heavier as the meal ended. John's brother and his family showed up, and dessert was served with great gusto. The Corey family took their sugar intake seriously. Yes, it was sad she couldn't stay here.

After the dessert plates were eaten clean so that not even a crumb remained of the delicious Boston cream pie John's brother's wife had brought, Alexandra retreated to the kitchen. Since she couldn't stay, she'd help out. She planned to be on the road heading south in an hour.

''What do you think you're doing, young lady?'' Bev scolded as she opened the freezer compartment of the stainless-steel refrigerator. ''You heard John. You're a guest. You have no business washing our dishes. Unless that means you're going to accept the job?''

Alexandra took one look at the hopeful crook of Bev's brow. ''Good try, but I'm only doing these dishes, as a good guest should in return for a delicious meal.''

"What about the ones in the oven?" Hailey clomped in, wearing her riding boots and her cowboy hat askew on her head.

Bev frowned. "Don't tell me he's back to doing that." She marched over to the oven and yanked on the door. "Out of sight, out of mind."

Hailey clomped close to inspect the mess. "Ew. They're all gross."

"Okay, maybe John needs hired help more than I think."

"That John." Bev shook her head. "If he keeps hiding them, how am I supposed to find them to wash?"

"You're not supposed to be washing my dishes." John strolled in, carrying a stack of dishes from the table outside. "That's why I hide 'em."

"No way, Dad. You hide 'em because *you* don't want to do 'em. That's what you said last night."

"I'm pleading the Fifth." John set the plates on the counter, so close Alexandra could feel his presence, tangible as a touch, as powerful as a tornado rolling over her.

It's a good thing this is a one-sided reaction, Alexandra thought as she swiped a stoneware plate beneath the faucet and slid it into the dishwasher rack. She'd had enough of romantic entanglements for now. Especially with men who looked too good on the outside.

He's a decent man at heart, too.

That truth bugged her big-time as she rinsed and stacked. She and Bev talked about gardening and the choir. But was it her fault her gaze kept straying to the open glass doors where John was?

Maybe it never hurt to look at a handsome man. Maybe, after the emotional pain Patrick caused her, she needed to see that other men were different. See how gentle John was? She paused, leaving the water running, while she watched him swing his five-month-old nephew into the air, just high enough to make the infant squeal with delight.

He's a good father. He probably wanted a lot of children. How sad he never got the chance.

"You want another one of those, I can tell," Tom, his brother, was saying as Alexandra bent to fill the soap dispenser with lemony dishwashing powder. His deep voice was so like John's, and carried just right, she couldn't help listening.

"This little guy's great, but you know good and well that I'm not going to marry again."

"You never know what God has in store for you," Tom reminded him.

"Broken hearts do mend, John," Nina, Tom's wife, reminded kindly as she took her son into her arms.

They were ganging up on him again. Hurt, he kept quiet. Tom and Nina had everything. They didn't understand. Broken hearts did mend, but not broken souls. Not easily, anyway. John smoothed the palm of his hand over little David's head, the finest silk of baby hair like a blessing against his skin. He and Bobbie had always wanted a big family. It was his fault they'd never gotten the chance.

Closing down the guilt and regret that raged like a century's storm, John turned away, making his excuses, but before he left he caught the look of pity on his sister-in-law's face. The sorrow on his brother's.

John, you still have a life, Tom had said on more than one occasion, and it was as if he was saying it now. John could feel it. He was ashamed, because no one in his family knew what had really happened. He'd tried to tell them at the time, but they'd made excuses. Hadn't wanted to see his failures. Not their oldest son, who'd never failed them. They couldn't believe he was responsible for his wife's death. And couldn't understand why he never deserved another chance at love.

That's the reason he tried to keep his gaze firmly fixed on the floor ahead of him and not straying toward the kitchen. Alexandra was wiping down the counters with an efficient swipe of her slender arm, her chestnut-brown braid bobbing between her shoulder blades as she worked. She looked young and vulnerable. Wisps of escaped hair curled around the faint bumps of vertebrae in her neck. Look how fragile she was.

Hadn't he vowed not to look at her? Angry with himself, John stormed through the family room and up the stairs, taking refuge as the silence of the second story closed around him. Sunlight streamed into the stained-glass windows at the end of the hallway, staining him with green and blue light as he stood gripping his forehead. What on earth was wrong with him?

He hadn't been able to stop noticing Alexandra across the table during the meal. The way she broke her biscuit into small bite-size pieces with her long, delicate fingers, those slim silver rings catching the light, as if to draw his gaze. The way she watched his family talk and banter and even argue over a meal, while her food went mostly untouched. As if a happy, extended family gathered together was a new experience for her.

That made him wonder more about her. What kind of family did she grow up in? Why wasn't she married? What had she left behind her? Where was she from?

Not his business. Still, it troubled him as he dug through the shelves in the extra room. Troubled him because he'd had his chance and blown it. He had no one to blame but himself. God wasn't going to trust him with anything so precious and sacred—not again. Nor would he trust himself.

There it is. He grabbed the battered copy of the travel guide and dusted it off with his sleeve. He stepped over a pile of magazines on the floor, cornered a toppling stack of newspapers and closed the door behind him. He was thinking about Alexandra way too much. Not a good sign. He would work harder to keep his mind where it belonged, give her the book and wave when she drove away.

A part of him didn't want her to drive away. What would it be like if she did stay?

Disaster. Don't even think like that, John. He grimaced, taking the stairs two at a time.

There, washed in sunlight and tousled by a gentle wind, Alexandra was laughing, with Hailey wrapped around her waist in a hug. He skidded to a stop in his tracks, right in the middle of the doorway. Hailey released her, hopping up and down as she always did, taking Alexandra by the hand and tugging her along the deck railing toward the back steps.

Alexandra was protesting, but not really meaning it. Hailey hauled her over to the lawn, where Bandit was waiting, reins dragging, ears pricked, long tail twitching.

"I really can't ride," Alexandra was saying. "I

never had a pony when I was a little girl. I'd fall right off.''

''You just gotta sit up straight. Don't worry. I'll show ya!'' Hailey grabbed the stirrup. ''See? It's easy. Just put your foot right in here.''

''Why don't you get up and show me first?'' Alexandra couldn't hide the quiver of panic in her voice.

Full of grace, she was, and all beauty. The wholesome kind, the way a sun rose over the Bridger Range. The kind of beauty that gave rest to a man's soul.

The man who wound up with Alexandra for his wife would sure be lucky.

''See?'' Hailey stretched on tiptoe to grab the saddle horn. ''You just do this, and then hop real high. See? I'm up.'' Hailey eased into the saddle. ''Wanna try?''

''Show me how you steer, first.'' Alexandra crossed her arms around her middle, the fear retreating. Maybe she figured once Hailey was on her horse she would stay there and forget about teaching Alexandra.

Wrong. Amused, John watched as Hailey rolled her eyes. ''You don't steer a horse like a car. You guide him. Like this.''

It was evident that Alexandra liked children. A lot. There was no hiding it on her face or the mirth that made her dark eyes twinkle. She'd be good for Hailey. The thought whispered through his mind, as if born on the breeze, carried straight from heaven. Hire her.

Well, that would be a mistake. Right?

"Well, son." Mom planted her elbows on the rail beside him. "How are we going to get her to change her mind?"

"We aren't." John figured God knew what He was doing. "She's made her decision."

"Yes, but look how Hailey adores her. Alexandra's good with children, with that gentle nature of hers." Bev fell silent.

Alexandra's gentle nature. That's all John saw. The quiet murmur of her laughter as she failed to hop high enough to climb into the saddle and slid back down to the ground. The veiled look of panic she tried to hide when she finally sat awkwardly in the saddle, staring at the ground in horror. The tranquil music of her voice as she commented, "Boy, that's a long way to fall. It's higher up here than I thought it would be."

Is this a sign, Lord? In one glance John took it all in—his precious daughter and Alexandra astride the little pinto. The rich land that rolled gently out of sight, the beauty of the mountains rimming the valley in all directions. The big house he could afford, and a loving extended family.

Why he'd been blessed so much, he didn't know, but one thing was for sure. Alexandra wasn't as fortunate in life. She was alone, and hurt shone in her eyes. A hurt he understood.

He had great debts to pay, and not of the financial kind. So what if he was attracted to Alexandra— nothing would come of it. The important thing was that the Lord had brought her to his doorstep, a vulnerable young woman in need. This was his chance to make another payment on the enormous debt he owed God. The answer to the same prayer he prayed every night.

The chance to make amends. To earn forgiveness for the unforgivable.

John knew exactly what he had to do.

Chapter Six

"**D**on't forget this." John's voice rumbled in Alexandra's ear as he dropped a battered book on the kitchen counter. "What are you gonna do? Just sneak off without saying goodbye?"

"No." Although she wanted to. It would sure be easier. "Your mom doesn't seem to want me to leave. And Hailey. She thinks I'm going to stay and take care of her. I'm not naming names, but I suspect someone is hoping that will change my mind."

"Hey, don't look at me. Hailey eavesdrops. It's terrible."

"But you're not, of course."

"Of course not. I would never try to use my daughter's affections to influence your decision." But his look said everything. "I pay well."

As if that were the only objection. Alexandra gazed around the kitchen, large and friendly and gorgeous. It sure would be a pleasure to cook in this kitchen. To spend her days looking after Hailey. "I do like your daughter."

"Ha! A victory. Does this mean you'll do it?"

"No. It means I'd love to, but I can't." Forget that one of the biggest reasons she couldn't accept was standing in front of her in living color, flesh and blood, too good to be true. "I wish it could be different."

"You'd like to stay?"

"Like to stay? I'd love to. Your family has been great to me. I can't remember the last time I felt so welcome anywhere."

"Then it's a sign from above." John smiled at her in that easy way he had, not flirtatious or coy, as he yanked open the refrigerator door. "Just say yes."

"I can't." She took a deep breath. Did she risk telling him?

"Okay, then what will make it easier for you to say yes? How about free room and board?" An ice-cream carton thunked to the countertop next to her. "Think about all that means. Free ice cream."

He lifted the lid, revealing rich chocolate, gooey fudge and fluffy marshmallow.

"Tempting."

"Bribery by chocolate. I knew it would work." He dug a scoop out of a drawer. "How about a sundae to celebrate your new job?"

"Hold the chocolate sauce. I haven't accepted yet." Alexandra took a deep breath. Did she trust John with the truth? Or did she run out of here the way she'd left Seattle, determined never to look back?

"Alexandra!" Hailey rushed in, cowboy hat hanging down her back. "I heard! You're gonna take care of me. I knew it!"

Reed-thin arms flung around Alexandra's midsection and squeezed so tight. Innocent and vibrant and so incredibly sweet. What a treat to be able to take care of Hailey as a job. She couldn't think of a nicer way to spend her days.

There were more reasons to leave than to stay. Patrick was one of them.

John was another. What was she going to do about the fact that she was attracted to him? Well, she could keep her distance. If she worked for him, then she was bound to be alone with him eventually.

Hailey grabbed a cookie and skipped out the door, chanting "yippee-skippy" over and over until she was out of sight, and out of hearing range.

John scooped fat rounds of ice cream into a half dozen bowls. "Want to start negotiating your wage?"

"Not yet." She took a deep breath, unable to put it off any longer. John had to know the truth *before* he hired her. "I have something to tell you first. Listen, and then you decide."

"Go on. I'm listening."

"A week ago I packed my camping gear and two bags of clothes in the dead of night and drove away from my apartment and my job and everybody I knew. I'm not aimlessly looking for work. I'm running for my life."

Running for her life? Was she in danger? There was no way she was in trouble with the law. It wasn't that kind of trouble.

He hazarded a guess. "Are you married?"

"No." She shook her head hard enough so the cinnamon-brown braid of hair slipped like silk over her delicate shoulders. "He was my fiancé."

"Was he violent? Did he hurt you?"

Alexandra didn't answer. She didn't have to.

She bowed her head. The silken wisps escaped from her braid fell forward, hiding her face, caressing the curve of her cheek. Her silence was more telling than a thousand words could.

Fury punched through him, and he shoved away from the counter, pacing hard, hands fisted. Seeing red, it was all he could do to control his anger. What kind of man hurt a woman? What sort of coward would terrorize someone half his size?

It was no Christian way to think, but he couldn't stop the wild surge of protective fury that tore through him like a rampaging flood. Drowning him so that he was sputtering for air, for control. No man had the right to do that to a woman. Especially one as good and gentle as Alexandra.

For her sake, he reined in his anger. He still shook with it, but raging at a faceless coward who wasn't even in this room wasn't going to help the ashen-faced, lost-looking woman who was staring at him with wide, worried eyes.

"You don't have to run another step. You'll be safe here." That was a promise he meant all the way to his soul. He knew it. God knew it. Alexandra would know it.

"He could be following me. He made threats."

"He won't find you. And if he does, I'm good friends with the town sheriff." John would talk to Cameron Brisbane first thing tomorrow. Cam was a good man. He'd be more than happy to help. With two of them keeping an eye out, Alexandra would be sure to be safe.

"But if Patrick found me, I could be putting Hailey in danger without knowing it. Or you." She held her chin up, a little wobbly, betraying her fear. "Maybe staying isn't the best idea. I had planned to get as far away as I could. Maybe go back East. I don't know."

"Thousands of miles won't keep you safe, not if he wants to find you." John uncurled his hands. Forced the rest of his muscles to relax. He'd seen enough as a member of the rescue team that he knew exactly what Alexandra was running from. He remembered a local domestic violence situation two years ago. He'd been called in to help find the missing wife.

And had found her body instead.

"It's not right to involve you by staying." Her chin lifted a notch higher. All strength and pride and courage. "This is my problem."

"Now it's mine, too. If two friends share a problem, then it's half the trouble."

She tried to frown at him, but ended up almost smiling instead. "Your ice cream is melting."

"Trying to divert me from the truth." He grabbed the carton and snapped the lid into place. "Too bad. It won't work. You're staying."

"Playing the boss already, are you?"

"Sure, why not? Just as long as you don't go running off alone. You have friends here." He shoved the carton blindly into the freezer compartment, hoping there was enough room on the rack. He knew what he had to do. "You don't need to be alone."

"You hardly know me. I hardly know you."

"I'm at the store all day, while you'd be here with Hailey. You'd be answering to my mom, mostly."

"Really?" She sounded cautious, but he could read her interest. She had an open heart that was easy to read and with hurt that was easy to see.

He hated that she was hurting so much down deep. Hated the horrible man who'd done this to her, made her feel unsafe and unable to trust a Christian man offering her a job—just a job. And nothing more.

The anger returned, but he forced it away. She surprised him by reaching out. The soft warm brush of her fingertips against his rough, sun-browned fingers unnerved him. Knocked him off balance and made him forget how to speak. She twisted the jar from his grip, sauntering away with a feminine gait that was simple and innocent and so womanly, he could only stare.

Lord, You've given me a woman to protect and defend. I'm up to this challenge. Really. John knew in his heart it wasn't going to be easy.

He was attracted to her. It was the plain and simple truth. He was a man. One day a woman was bound to come along and stir up feelings. It was only natural. That didn't mean he needed to acknowledge those feelings. Or act on them. Or give them a fraction of control over his life.

He had self-control. That's what mattered. The

trouble was, he was going to have to stop noticing she was so beautiful and vulnerable and amazing.

No problem there. He wouldn't look at her.

Averting his gaze, he grabbed the butterscotch chips from the pantry. He could hear the rasp of the silverware drawer, the tinkle of flatware, the metallic twist of a metal lid coming away from the jar.

Having Alexandra in his kitchen was going to take some getting used to. He unwound the twist tie from the bag and laid it on the counter.

She dolloped a meager amount of chocolate topping over the first bowl of ice cream. "Is this enough?"

"We don't do anything halfway here. We go for the gusto." He took the jar and upended it. The thick syrup sluiced over the ice cream to form a thick, delicious glacier of chocolate. "Anything less than that, and the crowd gets cranky. My mild-mannered dad will throw his shoe at you."

"Then I'd better put on a lot of chips, right?" She reached across him for the bag, bringing with her the scent of sweet green apples.

Not that he was about to notice. "If there's not enough chips, Mom will refuse to bring potato salad next Sunday. She's tough when it comes to punishment."

"I'd hate to get you in trouble. Is this enough?"

"Wow, you're generous with the butterscotch."

He poured syrup over the last bowl. "You fit in here. You oughta stay. You seem to like being here so far, and we like having you. 'Do not forget to entertain strangers, for by doing so some people have entertained angels without knowing it.'"

Why did her heart crumple like that? "I'm no angel, John."

"Close enough."

She wasn't going to be tempted. But she knew, as he handed her a bowl with a long-handled spoon in it, that it was already too late.

Staying here had to be a big mistake. Alexandra could *feel* it. She could admit it—she liked being needed. Even if it was for a job and nothing more.

She'd have to examine her motives later. But for now, as she dug into the depths of her purse for her car keys, she had enough to keep her busy. Hailey was chattering away, telling her exactly when the school bus came in the afternoons and exactly where it dropped her off. Alexandra would be waiting, right?

"Absolutely. I wouldn't forget you." Alexandra found her keys and slung the leather purse strap over her shoulder. "What do you want to do first when you get home tomorrow?"

"Ride Bandit. You can come, too." Hailey clasped her hands in sheer delight. "You did real good for a first-time rider. Well, not really, but you tried real hard.''

''Are you kidding? It was a disaster. Maybe I'll do better next time.'' Trying to forget the way she kept sliding off the saddle, Alexandra grabbed the grocery sack of leftovers from the counter. ''I'll see you tomorrow.''

''Cool!'' Hailey leaped close, wrapped her arms around Alexandra's middle and squeezed tight. Then she was gone, calling over her shoulder, ''You're awesome!''

I'm really going to have a hard time trying not to fall in love with that little girl. What a pleasure it would be to take care of Hailey day after day.

As for John… Alexandra vowed not to think of that as she trailed through the beautiful house and out the front door where the evening was giving way to the gathering shadows. Twilight clung to the far horizon, drawing the warmth from the air but not from her.

The Corey family was wrapped up in their good-byes. So genuinely loving and happy. They didn't know what it meant to be alone. Not truly alone. Not so isolated and afraid that it felt as if the world were passing you by.

She unlocked her car door and set the sack of leftovers on the front seat. John and his brother were laughing over some private joke, a friendly sound that lifted on the sweet evening breeze and came straight to her.

John was going to be a problem. She kept noticing him. Out of the corner of her eye as she tucked her purse on the floor and straightened. He stood with his back to her, in the fingers of the long shadows from the mighty oaks lining the driveway, standing just outside the light.

He made her so...aware. Aware of the scent of the lilacs on the breeze. The cool blush of twilight air on her bare arms. The creak of the car seat as she settled onto it. The newsprint texture of the travel book's pages against her fingertips.

It was time to be on her way. Quick, while she could still be rational and could control her feelings. She was tired and road weary and grateful for a place to rest. For now until she decided to move on, Bev's guest cottage would be her home. And these people her temporary family.

After a good night's rest, things would be better. She really didn't feel attracted to John—not real attraction. So she didn't need to worry. Right? He was like a white knight, and what maiden wouldn't gaze upon him with admiration? That's all this was.

He was her employer, and she was not ready to trust another man with her life.

She started the engine and sat waiting until the family's goodbyes were done. *Show me this is the choice You mean for me,* she prayed, as she followed Bev's car into the gathering darkness. With the night surrounding her, and no stars in sight, she couldn't help feeling alone. Afraid. Unsettled.

Maybe accepting this job was the wrong thing to do. Patrick could be following her.

Had she made another life-altering mistake? There came no answer and no peace as she followed the unlit, bumpy road that led through the Corey property. No stars winked wisely, and the heavens were hidden, the sky shrouded in clouds. She felt as if no one was watching over her, although she knew it wasn't true.

Although later she turned to her Bible and read before falling asleep that night, tucked in the cozy bedroom in the little cottage, the feeling remained.

John counted himself lucky to have a view of the Bridger Mountains from his kitchen windows. He could watch the purple-gray curtain of night lift, giving way to the soft golden light of a new dawn. That could inspire a man, that's for sure. As long as he knew toward what he was aspiring.

Lifting the teakettle from the stove, he contemplated the reverent changes in the sky. Purple slipping away to the deepest blue-gray, and faint pinks highlighting the underbellies of long, paintbrush strokes of the silhouetted clouds. He poured the steaming water into the awaiting cup, and the scent of apple lifted on the steam—sweet apple. The scent reminded him of Alexandra.

She was going to be here soon. In this house. In this kitchen. He panicked. Yesterday he'd been short of obsessed with her, his gaze drawn to her like a nail to a magnet. Helpless to break away.

He carried the cup to the table, where a hardback novel lay open, a weighted bookmark holding the page. The chair creaked as he settled into it, seeing the faint shadow of his reflection on the uncurtained bay window. Sitting alone. Hair sticking straight up, wrinkled shirt hanging crooked. Behind him was a stack of dishes he'd retrieved from the second oven.

The panic was still there. Alexandra. He ought to be relieved he'd finally found a housekeeper he could depend on, but he wasn't relieved. He was terrified. He was incredibly attracted to her. To this woman the Lord had brought to his doorstep. John would not fail her. He'd be as true as the dawn, sure as the sky, as steady as the mountains.

Reaching for the sugar bowl, he caught sight of the pictures nailed to the wall, the faint glow of the small lamp reflected in the brass frames. Pictures of Hailey, mostly. He'd started a collection, the same way his mother had. One picture had Bobbie in it proudly displaying her newborn daughter from her hospital bed. She was weary with exhaustion but beaming with joy. Bright balloons sailed in the air behind her, and flowers jammed the nightstand behind her.

Remembering that day brought tears to his eyes. He didn't want to go back to those feelings. To the time he'd taken for granted. Back then he and Bobbie thought they had all the time in the world. They'd been wrong about a lot of things. Wrong about the kind of man he was. The kind of husband.

Lord, I would do anything to bring her back. To go back in time and change those last few seconds of her life. To find some way to save her. To try harder. Be more. To have held on to her when I thought I couldn't.

He'd loved Bobbie more than his own life back then. His love had changed over the years, become a distant fondness mixed with the terrible guilt he carried. He knew what it was like to cherish a woman.

So, how could any man bring harm to someone he loved? Gulping down the hot tea, trying to burn away the lump of emotion caught painfully in his throat, John couldn't understand. Alexandra was on the run, and she was afraid. Afraid for her life. Afraid of being hurt again. Afraid to trust in anyone. Whoever this Patrick was, he'd wounded her deep inside. Didn't he know how precious love was? How brief a life could be?

John slammed the empty cup onto the table, launching out of the chair, his hands fisted, helplessness filling him. What he'd give to have the warmth of a wife's love, the music of her laughter, the comfort of her arms.

But it was not to be. He had no one to blame but himself.

In a few hours, when Alexandra walked through his front door, he'd be ready for her. Polite. Professional. A man dedicated to doing the right thing. When he gazed upon her, he vowed not to see a beautiful woman who made him wish.

He'd see an answer to his prayer for forgiveness. Nothing more, and nothing less.

Chapter Seven

Things weren't any clearer in the morning, although it was a beautiful day, the golden rays of sun carpeting the stone walk all the way to John's front door. Reaching into her pocket, she took out the set of keys Bev had given her. Just in case John wasn't home, Bev had said.

It didn't look as though John was home. Relief slipped through her. She hadn't realized how tense she was over this. She rang the bell just in case. No one came to the door. Looked like she was in luck. John was gone, true to his word.

This job could work out, she realized, as she tested a key. It didn't fit, so she tried the second one. The bolt turned, and she twisted the knob. The house echoed around her as she stepped into the hallway.

Serenity gathered around her like a hug. This was a real home, filled with love. She wanted a home like this someday. Maybe it wouldn't be this lavish. It could be a single-wide trailer, for all she cared. She simply wanted *this* feeling. *This* contented peace.

Well, she couldn't stand here dreaming. John wasn't paying her to stand in his living room all day. Tucking her dreams away, she headed straight for the kitchen. He'd probably left instructions on the counter. That's what a lot of people did, in her experience.

She laid her purse on the center island, but there was no list of chores needing to be done. No instructions of any kind. The granite counter shone in the morning light, highlighting crumbs and dust and a sprinkling of sugar, probably spilled from Hailey's cereal bowl.

She decided to start with the dishes stashed in the oven. It would take only a second to load the dishwasher, and a few minutes to deal with the handwash items. Already feeling at home in the roomy kitchen, she found the last clean dishcloth in the bottom stack of drawers. She heard a noise the same moment she pushed in the drawer.

Was someone outside? John's house wasn't on the beaten path. Bev had an appointment in town this morning, so it couldn't be her. Gerald was out in the fields, busy with his farming. John was at work.

Maybe it was something else. She turned on the faucet, letting the water warm. Over the rush of the running water, she heard it again.

Someone was outside. Patrick?

Fear sluiced over her like cold rain. Shivering, her palms went damp against the edge of the counter. What had he said the last time he'd threatened her? *You can't run from me. You aren't smart enough. I'll hunt you down like a dog until I find you. Then you'll be sorry.*

It's him. Fear made her certain. She grabbed the phone with trembling hands, but what good would that do? She could call for help, but it would take a good twenty minutes for the police to come. She was in the middle of farmland and wilderness. She could try to run out the back, but what if Patrick was waiting for her? Her car was out front. He would already know she was here.

The front knob jingled and turned. The hinges whispered open. She heard the pad of a man's boot on the wood floor.

Frantic, she searched for something to defend herself with. She didn't know how to use a knife, so she didn't bother with that. There was nothing useful in the top drawers. She yanked open the pantry door and grabbed the first thing she saw. The wooden broom handle fit into her hand perfectly, and she held it steady. Just having it made her feel stronger. At least she had something to fight with.

What if Patrick had a gun? What good would a broom do her then?

The footsteps tapped closer. Leisurely. Quietly. As if he were listening for a sign of where she was in the house.

Adrenaline fired through her. Praying for guidance, Alexandra tiptoed to the wide entry that separated the spacious kitchen from the formal dining room. The footsteps were so close. Maybe if she struck first, she'd be able to knock him down. That would give her enough time to run to her car—

A shadow filled the doorway. It was now or never. Her entire life could depend on this. She swung like a batter over home plate, hoping to get him right in the stomach.

A big male hand curled around her, stopping the swing before it made contact with a very hard-looking, very solid-looking solar plexus. Patrick was a little portly, and this man was sheer muscle.

"Whew. That's what I get for not warning you before I step into a room." John released her hand and took the broom from her. "You have a good arm. There are local baseball teams who'd be proud to have you."

Had she really almost hit her employer? "John, I'm sorry. I was afraid you were someone else."

"The fiancé?" He lowered the broom. "That's all right. I'm glad to know at least you can defend yourself. Armed with a broom. Do you have a permit for this?"

"You're teasing me."

"Absolutely not. You could have broken a rib with the force of your swing. Wow. Come the next church picnic, I'm picking you for my team first off."

"Stop trying to make me feel better." Her face was burning. What did John think of her? She'd been ready to hit him. "Wait one minute. Aren't you supposed to be at work? You told me I'd never really see you. That I'd be answering to Bev."

"Right, well, I forgot this." He pulled a folded square of yellow notebook paper from his shirt pocket. "Went to the trouble of making up a list and then didn't leave it."

"I was looking for that." Her hands were shaky as she reached out for the note. There was no way to hide it, especially since the paper rattled in her unsteady grip. There was never a hole in the floor to sink into when you needed one.

"Hey, I really scared you. I'm sorry. Are you all right?" His fingers curled around hers, warm and strong and slightly callused against her skin. A strong hand, but he held her with infinite gentleness.

Gentleness she was afraid to believe in. It was too good to be true. She knew it down deep. She withdrew her hand, leaving him in the threshold, retreating to the sink where the water was still running. "Sure, I'm fine. Just easily startled, I guess. That's what I get for not locking the door behind me."

"It was my fault. You have every right to be afraid, considering what you've been through."

She didn't want his pity or his sympathy. And if he kept speaking to her in that quiet, steady voice, the one that sounded as genuine as the earth, as real as a kept promise, then she was going to be in big trouble. She grabbed a plate, ran it under the water and fit it into the bottom dishwasher rack.

"You don't have to rinse the dishes." He lifted the next plate from her grip and slipped it into the rack beside the first. "It's a top-of-the-line dishwasher. It'll clean the worst of this mess, no problem."

She felt foolish. Of course, he was right. Top-of-the-line. Just like everything else about his life. She should have known. Boy, this first day wasn't starting out well. "Good. Then I guess I'll get this load of dishes started faster. If I can reach the dishwasher."

"Oh, right." He stepped aside, all six substantial

feet of him. "I've got another stack of dishes hidden on the bottom shelf of the refrigerator behind the pizza boxes. Just thought you should know."

"You couldn't put them in the dishwasher yourself, huh?"

"That's right. It's a character defect men have called Dishwasher Avoidance."

"I've heard of that. Sort of related to Laundry Evasion."

"Exactly. I'm glad you understand."

"I'm a professional. It's my business to understand." Alexandra bit her lip. Okay, he was funny and she wasn't going to let herself encourage him with so much as the tiniest smile. How else was she going to keep her emotional distance? "I've got the list now. I'll be fine."

"The list. Right." He jammed his hands deep into his pockets. "I know you'll be fine. I spoke to the town sheriff. He says it would be best if you talked to him. Give him a description of this fiancé."

"Oh, John, I wish you hadn't done that." The last thing she wanted was for other people to know about this. That was the best way to expose a secret in a small town. "I only told you about Patrick because I thought you needed to know. Because of Hailey's safety. I didn't think you'd actually—"

She turned away, too angry to say anything more. Why had he done that? He'd probably thought he was helping. But he wasn't. Now she'd be easier to find.

"Cam will keep it off-the-record. Unofficial. No one will know." His hand lighted on her shoulder, his touch unshakable and solid. As dependable as the man. "He needs a description, so he can keep his eye out. He's on your side, Alexandra. Just like I am."

How could a stranger be on her side? Again, she didn't know what to say. In her experience, people had never been true to their word. Not when the chips were down. Not when it mattered. And the one time she'd thought differently...well, she couldn't have been more wrong.

"I can handle this on my own." She met his gaze, unflinching. Let him see that she wasn't as helpless as he apparently thought. "I appreciate the job, John, you know that. I'm grateful for the chance to stay with your family. But I don't need a white knight."

"I never thought you did." He didn't back down, didn't blink, didn't soften his voice. "But even a brave damsel can use help now and then."

"I'm not brave." She was living by faith. It wasn't always easy. Maybe she shouldn't have accepted this job. Maybe it had been a mistake. "If you don't think I can take care of myself, then are you worrying that I can't take care of Hailey?"

"Whoa. I wouldn't have offered you the job if I thought that." He grabbed an open box of tea left on the counter. "How about a peace offering? We'll sit down and clear the air. How about it?"

"I'm not sure I should associate with the enemy."

"I'm not the enemy. Just your employer. It's not the same thing." He waggled the box at her. "I've got a bowl of my mom's cookies I'll throw in for good measure."

"That's a good bargaining chip. It's a deal." She gazed up at him with a wariness that she tried to hide with the smallest curve of her lips, a smile that was strained.

She wasn't used to kindness. Maybe she'd stopped believing in it. The emotional pain an abusive relationship must exact on a woman must be enormous. John filled two cups with water and slipped them into the microwave.

As the unit hummed, he grabbed Mom's bowl of cookies and dropped them on the end of the counter that served as a breakfast bar. The way he saw it, maybe it was his job to help her to truly smile again.

The microwave beeped, and she brushed past him to whip the steaming cups out of the machine. She was industrious. He had to give her that. Hardworking, kind, she'd be good to Hailey. He couldn't get luckier when it came to a housekeeper. He'd been

looking hard for three weeks, and couldn't find anyone who was half as good.

That only proved to him that this was meant to
be.

He dropped two spoons on the marble counter. "I
trust you with my daughter. Just so you know."

"I wouldn't blame you if you didn't." She
climbed onto a stool, careful to leave an empty stool
between them, as if she was afraid of getting too
close.

Yep. She'd been real hurt. It was too bad. John's
heart squeezed with sympathy for her, a pain so
sharp he had to look away to hide it.

"Sometimes I feel like I can barely take care of
myself. I suppose I shouldn't confess that to you."
She took a tea bag from the box he offered her. Her
slim fingers tugged the end of the tea string, her
silver rings flashing, and she dunked the bag into
the steaming water. "Sometimes this is overwhelming. If I stop and think about it."

"Then my motto would be Don't Think About
It."

"Exactly what I'm trying to do. But then this man
wanted to hire me, and I had to admit the truth."

"Where is this man? I'll knock some sense into
him. Tell him you want to forget the past. Leave it
behind you."

"That would be good. Hey, where did that broom go?"

He chuckled. So, she could make him laugh. That didn't mean he was going to like her any more than he'd liked any other housekeeper. "Denial isn't just a river in Egypt, right?"

"It's my preferred state of mind."

"I've spent time there." He plunged his tea bag into the water and watched the liquid froth. The scent of apples and cinnamon warred with his senses. The tea smelled good, but it was nothing compared to Alexandra's sweetness. "You said you left everything behind. That had to be hard."

"I was renting a furnished room in a house, where we shared the kitchen and living areas. I didn't really have much, but I did leave most of what I had. I took my camping gear and two duffel bags of clothes."

She must have been in a lot of danger. "Did your housemates know what you were going to do?"

She shook her head, scattering her molasses-dark hair and making her earrings jangle. She appeared smaller on the chair. More fragile. "No one did. I'd cashed my paycheck that afternoon. Patrick had been watching me carefully, so I didn't want to do anything suspicious. Like closing my account. Packing my car up after work. That sort of thing."

"He was watching you? As in stalking you?"

Her fingers trembled as she wound the string around the tea bag, squeezing the liquid from it. "I'd already given him back his engagement ring. He didn't take it well."

"He wouldn't let you go? Was he violent?"

"He didn't think he had a problem with his anger while he was yelling at me." She kept her voice even, as if an angry yelling man was nothing to be afraid of.

John knew better. He could see it without her words. Sense it as if he'd been able to peek inside her heart. The secrecy of quietly packing one evening, windows closed, curtains drawn, a radio on to hide the noise of dresser drawers opening and metal hangers rocking on the wooden closet rod.

"You're going to be safe here." He resisted the urge to reach out and brush away the lines of worry from her brow with the pad of his thumb. He knew what it was like to be afraid. To hurt. To want peace. "I'm going to make sure of it."

"I can't ask that of you. I'm not even sure I should be here. I appreciate the job, don't get me wrong, and the pay is generous, but you're not my keeper."

"Someone has to be." John offered her the cookie bowl. "Just think of me and my family as your temporary guardian angels. We'll watch over you."

An uneasy chill shivered through her stomach. She kept her voice light, because not all men were like Patrick, right? John didn't mean he'd literally be keeping a watch on her. "A girl can't have too many angels looking out for her."

"Good. I'll have the sheriff drop by, so be expecting him. You won't be in need of the broom." He bit into the edge of the iced cookie.

"Thanks for mentioning that. I'm still embarrassed enough I could spontaneously combust."

"Why? It's important for a woman to know how to defend herself. Cameron will be able to keep an eye out for any strangers in town. With any luck, this Patrick of yours will decide to stay in Seattle where he belongs."

"That's what I'm hoping." She bit into the cookie and let the sweetness melt on her tongue. She thought of her self-esteem, still tender, and tried to put aside the bad memories of Patrick's angry words that always tore her down....

No, she wouldn't think of that ever again. She was strong enough to evade him. To make a new life. With the Lord watching over her and a few extra guardian angels, she couldn't go wrong.

"Didn't you get a restraining order? Didn't the police help you?"

"A restraining order can only do so much, and the police did all they could." She closed her mind against the pain. The wound in her heart hurt like crazy. She'd once loved Patrick Kline with all her being. Where all that love used to be was a dark, aching place that felt as if it would never be touched by sunlight again.

"You don't need a restraining order here. Not with me around." John's gaze met hers, full of promise, as unyielding as the strongest steel. "You're safe with me. You can count on it."

The tension inside her eased. Just like that, like a tangled knot of yarn suddenly pulling loose. She believed in him. "You really are a guardian angel."

"Good, I've got you fooled." With a wink, John slid off the stool with a man's athletic power, taking the mug and cookie with him. "I've been told I'm a good listener. Any time you want to talk, I'm here. You're not alone. Remember that."

"I will."

"If you have any questions about the list I gave you, just give me a jingle down at the store. I wrote down the number."

"Sure thing." It was hard to speak past the tight ball of emotions locked in her throat, but she managed.

He disappeared through the threshold, and his steps tapped through the house. The door opened, then closed, leaving silence in his wake.

For the first time in a long while, Alexandra didn't

feel alone. Her spirit had been uplifted after she'd confided in John. She hadn't dared to trust her troubles to many people. Opening up now left her feeling connected instead of isolated and reminded her that God's love was everywhere, especially in the hearts of others.

She took another bite of the delicious cookie and started reading the work list John had left her.

The late-afternoon sun was blazing strong enough to make the inside of the old VW hot as Alexandra pulled into the gravel driveway of the little yellow house a few blocks from the town's main street. It was always a blessing not to have air-conditioning. Otherwise how could she appreciate the sun's heat?

She killed the engine and rolled down the rest of the windows. A strain of piano music lilted from the house's open front door. Hailey's halting rendition of "Moonlight Sonata" was certainly unique. Fondness for the little girl filled Alexandra's heart right up.

What a wonderful day this had been. After a morning spent cleaning John's beautiful house, she'd met Hailey at the bus stop at the end of the mile-long driveway. Stephanie had come to visit, so there were two little girls to entertain. Easy to do with a fresh pitcher of lemonade and the last of Bev's Sunday cookies.

While she'd dusted the plant shelves in the family room, the sounds of their laughter and constant chatter wafted in through the open windows. Happy sounds of childhood that Alexandra remembered from other children's homes. From other children's yards.

She grabbed the dust mop, reaching for the peak of the vaulted ceiling, straining on the top step of the small ladder she'd found in the garage. Those happy, innocent voices drifting into the room made her happy, too. As if, for one moment in time, she was able to step out of the shadows of her troubles and let the sun warm her. It had been a good feeling, and it lingered with her still as she waited for Hailey's lesson to end.

The halting music continued, one wrong note souring the melody, and then another. She tugged a paperback inspirational romance out of her purse and opened it to the dog-eared page that marked her place. She'd no sooner started reading than she heard footsteps in the gravel behind her.

"Alexandra." It was John's voice and his reflection in the cracked side-view mirror, coming closer.

Oh, he looks good. That was her first thought. Her second was—don't notice. "John. Bet you couldn't resist the chance to hear your daughter play."

A series of sour notes came from inside the house before the melody rang true.

"I'm not sure her true talent is the piano, although Mom sure keeps hoping." John knelt down so they were eye level. "I was down the street delivering a new mower to the Whitlys, and I spotted your car."

Only then did she recognize the big red pickup parked across the street behind her. "Checking up on me?"

"Let's call it Providence lending a hand. The Whitlys have puppies that are just eight weeks old today. They offered me the pick of the litter, since I didn't charge them for the delivery."

"Now you're in a bind—is that it? Seeing as Hailey wants a dog."

"You see my situation. If I say no, then I'm a horrible, terrible father of the worst sort. If I say yes, then I've got a puppy in my house."

"Look at the bright side. You have wood floors and not carpeting. That will come in handy during housebreaking."

"I like your outlook on life. Yep, there's a blessing if I ever saw one." He shook his head, scattering his dark hair, and for a moment those shutters on his soul opened again. It was easy to see all the good in him.

When he caught her looking at him, the shutters closed. She felt embarrassed for looking so deep.

John stood, gazing at the house, feeling distant

again. Remote. "Think you're up to coming along and helping us pick out a dog?"

Before Alexandra could answer, the old metal screen door flung open and a pink-and-purple blur streaked out of the house.

"Daddy!" the streak shouted in an excited rush. "What dog? I getta dog? Yippeeeeee! I'm gonna get a dog. Really, really, truly?"

"Nope. Just kiddin'." John's wink brought another squeal as Hailey bounded to a stop against Alexandra's car, jumping up and down with glee.

"What kind of a dog? A baby one, right? It's the Whitlys' babies, isn't it? I *knew* it. My best friend Christa lives next door and she gets to visit them sometimes. She wants to get the white one, but I ain't never seen them even once—"

Hailey kept talking, and John held up one hand, like a crossing guard attempting to halt speeding traffic. "It's not doing any good."

"I see that." Alexandra covered her mouth to hide her laughter.

"You see why I hired you? I need help."

"If I had known that, I'd have demanded higher wages."

"Maybe hazard pay." John took his daughter by the shoulders and guided her around to the passenger side door, while she chattered the entire time.

He opened the door and Hailey plopped into the seat, chasing away all the quiet.

"I won't want the white one, 'cuz it's the one Christa likes, but maybe there'll be one I like. Do you know what? What if there isn't one I like?"

"With my luck, you'll like all of them. Don't worry." John brushed tangles from her face, a wonderfully loving fatherly gesture, before handing her the seat belt. "Buckle up, and give Alexandra directions. I'll follow, okay?"

"Yep. I love you, Dad." She gave him a smacking kiss on the cheek, an open show of affection that made Alexandra look away.

She turned the key, pumping the gas until the old engine sputtered to life. She felt sharply alone, even with Hailey's merry chatter and John waving them off as she backed onto the street.

"Yippee! I get a dog. I really, really get one. Can you believe it? Cool. My dad's so cool." Hailey bounced on the seat, her happiness tangible. She beamed, her hands clasped, all brightness and innocence.

"Your dad is definitely cool." Alexandra could see him in the rearview, walking the half block down the residential street, his athletic gait striking, his hair wind tousled. There was something about him that held her attention—and that couldn't be good.

Don't think about it.

She forced her attention completely on the road ahead of her, following Hailey's pointing finger toward a paved driveway in front of a vintage, Craftsman-style house, where a profusion of bright tulips were cheerfully saluting.

An elderly woman rose from her weeding in the colorful flower beds in the shade of the house, and waved her garden-gloved hand. Her face wreathed into a smile. "Why, it's Hailey. Your daddy said we ought to be expecting you."

"Hi, Mrs. Whitly!" Hailey shot from the car before Alexandra could set the brake.

Alexandra then pocketed her keys, approaching, as the older woman offered a friendly greeting.

"I saw you in church," Mrs. Whitly was saying, grasping Alexandra's hand in a tight hold that felt so sincere. "What a blessing you are to them, I'm sure. That poor widower all alone, and with a child to raise. I already sent Hailey into the house to find the puppies on her own. Didn't think that child could wait a second longer without exploding on the spot."

"Good idea. She's pretty excited."

"So I see." Laughing, Mrs. Whitly held open the door. "Please come in. Can I get you some iced tea?"

"Thank you." Being part of the Corey family

made her belong somehow, she figured. Small towns were like that, she knew all too well. It was a nice privilege, to be welcomed without question.

"Go on into the laundry room." Mrs. Whitly gestured to the far end of her perfectly tidy kitchen to an open door, where Hailey sat sprawled on the linoleum floor, surrounded by leaping puppies.

"Alexandra! Look!" Hailey twisted around, hugging one fluffy black puppy beneath her chin, sparkling like all the stars in the sky, like joy unleashed.

In all her life, Alexandra had never been so happy, but it touched her now. Knocked away one stone in the wall around her heart. Forgetting that she was an adult and not a child, she fell to her knees amid the puppies, scooping up a wiggling little brown one that jumped right into her hand.

"He's so soft." She'd never felt anything so wonderful. Fluffy puppy paws were everywhere—her arms, her shoulders, on her jeans, as the little ones tried to get her attention, jumping up to swipe wet warm tongues at her chin.

"I love this one!" Hailey kissed the head of the puppy she cradled. "This one is the sweetest, bestest puppy, right?"

"Right." Alexandra started when a hand lighted on her shoulder. A heavy, broad touch that somehow made the happiness inside her double. Made another brick crumble in the wall around her heart.

John knelt down beside her. "It looks to me like these puppies are all wrong. Now that you girls have looked, let's leave them and go."

"Daddy!" Hailey protested, giggling. "I found the one I want. Looky!"

"I was afraid of that." John winked, acting as if he was greatly pained, but anyone could see the happiness that made him bigger than life. "Looks like you've got yourself a dog, Hailey."

"I know." She said it with such confidence, as if there had never been a single doubt in her mind. She'd known all along how this would work out.

Alexandra turned away, lowering the puppy she held to the floor, stroking its downy little head with her fingertip. A second pup pushed its way in, wanting attention, too.

All her life, she'd been on the outside looking in. Like a child peeking through the window, wistfully wishing to be part of the happy family inside. She'd always wondered if those people she saw were really that happy. Or was it different, with the curtains drawn and the doors closed. Were they as unhappy down deep as her family had been?

It had always burdened her. She wanted to marry. She wanted a family, just like the ones she'd always watched so wistfully as a child while at the same time fearing that nothing could be that wonderful. Not really.

And now she knew for sure. Those families were real. Like John's family. So this dream in her heart *could* really happen—one day. Maybe that was why God had brought her here, on this uncertain journey from her past. To show her this genuine, happy family. To let her see what her future could be.

She hugged another puppy close, closed her eyes and gave a silent prayer of thanks.

Chapter Eight

"I hope you know something about dogs."

Alexandra dug her car keys out of her pocket. "Actually, I do, but you're not paying me for that."

"Getting tough with me, are you?" He crossed his arms over his chest, impressive as always with the shadows clinging to him and the wind ruffling his dark hair. "I knew you were too good to be true. Now I see the real Alexandra."

"Oh, you're one to talk. Hiring me to keep house and look after your daughter, and now this. A hidden agenda."

"Guilty as charged. Except I didn't know we were going to get a dog so soon."

"You must have known you would fold and give in to Hailey's wishes. After all, Mrs. Whitly told me you had asked about the puppies only last week."

"Can't trust anyone to keep a secret. What's the world coming to? Okay, so I had a suspicion, but that's all it was. Mom doesn't know anything about dogs, either, so that leaves us at your mercy."

"You're in luck. I do have some puppy knowledge, but it's going to cost you."

"I knew you were going to say that. Okay, give it to me. How much is this going to set me back?"

"Your mom's potato salad recipe. Hey, don't look at me like that. I know what's important in life."

"Getting you all the gold in Fort Knox would be easier. Do you know my mom guards that secret family recipe with her life? Is there any chance I could just pay you extra?"

"Nope." Alexandra swung her car door open. "Talk to Bev."

"She's gonna hurt me if I ask her for the recipe."

"A big brave man like you shouldn't be afraid of a little pain." She couldn't help teasing. "Still want my help with the puppy?"

He gestured toward the pickup's passenger window where Hailey could be seen through the tempered glass, her cheek to the puppy's cute round head. They were nuzzling, clearly in love, as only little girls and their puppies can be.

"I need all the help I can get," John confessed. "Are you going to make me beg?"

"It's tempting, but I'll spare you this time." Alexandra dropped her purse on the floor. "I'll follow you to the grocery store."

"You're going to have fun spending my money, aren't you?"

"We'll just pick up a few things the puppy needs for tonight, but there's a pet store in Bozeman that could be making a profit tomorrow."

John's fist flew to his heart, as if she'd inflicted a mortal wound. "I'll take it like a man and give you my credit card."

"And how exactly am I going to use your credit card without being arrested for fraud?"

"I know the owner of the pet store. I'll give him a call first thing in the morning."

"Good." She tossed him a smile that could charm the sun out of the sky and slipped behind the wheel of her rusted yellow VW.

Slim and lithe, as graceful as dreams, she lifted her delicate hand in a wave, silver rings flashing, before backing out of the driveway.

"I love you, puppy, yes I do. You're so cute," Hailey cooed, touching noses with the tiny fluffy black dog that gazed up at her with sheer love in those chocolate eyes.

Trouble. That's all John saw as he pulled out onto the street. Next thing he knew the dog would be sleeping with Hailey. And then it was going to be on the furniture. He'd no longer be king of his own castle. The dog would be. Well, queen, since she was a female.

Maybe it wouldn't be so bad. He reached over to rub a hand over the puppy's warm downy back. A pink tongue darted out in a quick, grateful caress. Okay, so maybe he wasn't gonna mind too much.

"I'm gonna need a girl name. A real name," Hailey chattered on over the Christian country station humming in the background. "Something really pretty, just as pretty as my cute baby puppy."

John ruffled her hair, too, and made her laugh. "I have every confidence you'll come up with the best name."

"Well, yeah, Daddy. I'm good." Hailey stared deeply into her puppy's eyes. "How about Ariel? Nope. I know. Alexandra."

"That would get awful confusing with two Alexandras in the same house."

Hailey sighed, exasperated. "I know. Danielle. Nope."

John eased up on the gas. He hadn't realized he'd been speeding, and he'd already caught up with the time-faded yellow Beetle puttering along the road in front of him. He could just barely see Alexandra's cinnamon-dark hair. It was fluttering around her shoulders, whipped by the wind through the open windows.

She's so different from Bobbie.

Where that thought came from, John didn't know, but he didn't like it. He was Alexandra's protector. That's what he was. He had no right watching the flick of her long hair in the breeze and seeing a woman instead of his duty. His chance to make amends.

"Belle." Hailey tilted her head to one side, contemplating that name. "Belle? Here Belle, girl?"

The puppy kept licking Hailey's chin.

There was traffic in town, since it was nearly quitting time. He pulled up in a space next to Alexandra in front of the grocery. If he leaned out the window, he could make out the hardware store—looked like Warren was just closing up.

"Hey, I'll run in and grab some puppy food." Alexandra leaned against the passenger side window, reaching through to stroke the puppy's soft head.

Her silver rings flashed, drawing his gaze as they always did. Small and fragile hands. So unlike Bobbie, who'd been strong and capable and athletic. Always the tomboy.

Right there showed how wrong he was. If the day ever came when he'd paid enough for Bobbie's death, he wouldn't want a wife so fragile. So delicate. So easily hurt.

He pulled his wallet out of his back pocket,

opened it and handed her a twenty. "Will that be enough?"

"For now." Her smile dazzled. She dazzled.

He held his heart steady, refusing to feel anything at all.

"Here, Daddy. Hold Jessica." Hailey handed him the beloved puppy. "Nope. That's all wrong."

"Don't worry." Alexandra's soft, sweet alto rang like the gentlest hymn. "I bet she'll name herself. Trust me."

Hailey put her hand in Alexandra's, and the two trotted off, the taller, beautiful woman and the beloved little girl, and disappeared from his sight.

"John, do you have any more newspaper?" Alexandra breezed into his kitchen, breathless and flushed, a smile shaping her soft mouth. "I'm afraid the puppy has used what I could find on the shelf."

"There's the recycling bin in the garage."

"There is? I didn't see it." She flicked on the oven light and peered inside. "Looks like another ten minutes will do it. Let me get the puppy settled, and I'll set the table for you."

"Your shift ended an hour ago. I'll take care of it. And the newspaper, too."

"Are you sure?"

"It's about time I'm good for something." He winked, forcing a smile.

"Hmm. You seem to be useful at making your daughter very happy." She smiled like a ray of sunlight on a bleak day, warming him straight through. Unaware of her effect on him, she disappeared down the hallway.

What was bothering him? He couldn't put his finger on it. Whatever it was, it had his stomach in knots.

Was it the way she looked? No, because he'd hardly noticed she was wearing well-worn Levi's and a baggy purple T-shirt with the University of Washington in faded gold letters. He *wasn't* attracted to her—absolutely not. He was in control of his feelings.

Something was bugging him, though. When he figured out what it was, then he'd be able to solve the problem. He wasn't going to worry about it until then.

He grabbed three plates from the cupboard and dealt them around the table. Alexandra might as well stay and eat with them, since she'd stayed late. It was the decent thing to do, a gesture a man who considered himself her protector would make.

It had nothing to do with the fact that she was an extremely attractive woman. Because he simply wasn't noticing.

When he was done at the table, he headed straight for the garage, grabbed a bundle of newspapers from the bin. On the way through the house, he couldn't help noticing the changes Alexandra had already made. The floors shone. The furniture was vacuumed and plumped and tidier. The big-screen television was dust free.

Hey, now there was an improvement. He'd like that the next time the Mariners were playing. No more screen lint.

Feminine giggles trilled like music down the hallway, drawing him closer. Hailey's high bright laughter blended with Alexandra's quieter, deeper chuckle, and that chuckle seemed to be the most wonderful sound he'd ever heard.

"No, puppy, you're supposed to go on the paper." Hailey started to giggle harder. "Alexandra, she's goin' again."

"She's going to be just fine once we're not in here with her." Alexandra was folding an old towel, made soft by wear, into a cozy piece of bedding. "She'll probably cry for a while, because she'll be lonely, but she'll settle in."

"The teddy bear will help." Hailey placed one of her favorite stuffed animals from years ago into the big cardboard box that was now stuffed with so much bedding, there was no room for the puppy. "Maybe she shouldn't sleep by herself. She's awful little."

Yep, here it comes. The plea to have the puppy

in her bedroom. John braced himself, prepared to hold out for as long as he could—probably two hours tops. "The newspaper you requested."

"Just in time. The last of it has been properly used." Alexandra snatched the bundle from him and dove into it, hard at work, her hair falling down to curtain her face, so all he saw was the part going straight down the middle of her head.

There was something about that part in her hair. The way the fine line of porcelain skin was a contrast to the rich brown strands. Something that made him forget that she was vulnerable and alone and in trouble, and it was his job to protect her and instead made him notice she was all woman, grace and poetry.

Stop noticing her, John.

Her slender fingers tucked a satiny lock of her hair behind her ear, revealing the soft curve of her cheekbone and the elegant shape of her small chin. Her bow-shaped mouth curved into a laughing smile as the puppy leaped up on her and then crashed down in the middle of the newspaper she was trying to unfold.

The sharp rustle of newsprint made the tiny creature yip with delight, her tiny, furry body wiggling from head to tail.

"Look at her. She's so cute." Hailey got down on all fours. "I love you so much. Yes, I do."

The little puppy leaped up to touch noses with her.

That was simply too much sweetness for a man to take. John swallowed hard, trying not to feel too much of anything. Sometimes it could be so overwhelming, all this he'd been given, this daughter he treasured, this life he lived, the moments like this that were tiny pieces of forever.

"I'd best go check on supper." He moved away from the sounds of laughter and crackling newspaper and the puppy's yips of delight.

It was only when he was setting the casserole dish on the trivet in the middle of the table that it hit him what was wrong. It hit him as hard as a plane crashing down from the sky to the earth. As desolating as the fire and flame and metal tearing apart on impact.

His knees gave out, his feet went out from under him and he landed in a chair, clinging to the edge, struggling for breath.

This is what it had been like when Bobbie was alive. The low murmur of a woman's voice down the hall. The bright feminine presence changing the house in some vital, undeniable way that could only be felt by the soul.

In a way, that made new all the pain of the past, all the regret and anguish, as if the void in his life had been ripped open again, and there was no energetic Bobbie zipping around this kitchen, laughing while she worked.

There was Alexandra. And he was glad for that.

He'd had housekeepers before, but it had never been like this. He'd never really been in the house at the same time as those other women—young or old—who'd worked afternoons keeping watch over Hailey and his home.

He hadn't realized taking Alexandra into his life would bring him here, to this place of bleak, burning pain.

The grief was over, but not the guilt. It hit him with the force of an inferno, leaving him weak and sweating, consumed and empty all at once.

He had to find a way to pull himself together.

"What about Maggie? I sorta like Maggie." Hailey's voice echoed through the house—she was in the hallway, coming closer.

John realized his cheeks were wet and he swiped the dampness away. After a few deep breaths his knees held him up when he straightened from the chair.

Just in time. Hailey bounded around the corner, tugging Alexandra by one hand. Alexandra shone, as if the armor she'd been hiding behind had been peeled back, to expose a truer, more open part of her.

It was like looking at her for the first time.

"Oh, no." Alexandra glanced over her shoulder, her cinnamon-brown locks tumbling everywhere, catching the light, catching his heart.

It's because I can help her, when I failed Bobbie. That's why I feel this way. John clung to that, determined to push away every other feeling until the pain and the anguish were gone. His hands still shook, though, when he rescued the salad from the refrigerator.

"Is the puppy all settled?" At least he could keep his voice steady.

"Yep." Hailey dropped into her chair, unaware, as bouncy as ever. "Alexandra said I couldn't bring a dog to the table."

"Probably not a good idea for tonight." John kept his gaze firmly fixed on the tray in the refrigerator door that held the bottles of salad dressing. He grabbed both of them—Ranch for Hailey and Italian for him. Maybe Alexandra would like either one—

There he went thinking of her again. But only in the protective, most noble of ways.

"I should probably head out." Her voice, and the pad of her step on the floor behind him. "I'll leave you two to your dinner."

"Don't think you're getting out of here that easy." He hit the fridge door with his foot. "You made dinner. You should help eat it. It's only fair. What if the casserole tastes bad?"

"You need an official taste tester, is that it?"

"No. We need a guinea pig to make sure your casserole doesn't make us sick."

"If I don't keel over, then you'll risk it?"

"Exactly. It didn't look so good when I took off the lid. Scary."

Hailey repositioned herself, clambering onto her chair with both knees to get a good look at the questionable casserole. "It does not, either, Dad! It's all cheesy. It smells good."

"Smells can be deceiving." He winked.

There he went again, making her laugh, making her troubles disappear like dandelion fluff on the wind. "Fine. I'll be the royal taste tester, since you need one."

"Knew you'd see things my way."

"I'll warn you. This is my favorite recipe, so if you don't like it, I'll have to raid your mom's recipe box. Wouldn't it be too bad if I ran across the potato salad recipe?"

"Dream on." John set the bottles on the table. "It's such a secret, it's not written down. Mom's committed it to memory and will only reveal the great truths of it when she's on her deathbed. Or so she swears."

"Hmm. Getting that recipe is going to be a challenge." Undaunted, Alexandra stowed her purse and took one of the extra chairs at the table.

A terrible, high-pitched wail careened through the house and echoed in the rafters above.

"What is that?" John boomed like a clap of thunder. "Is that the *dog?*"

Alexandra shrank. She couldn't help it. He was a big man, wide and strong, bounding out of his chair as if the house were on fire.

His big hands closed into lethal fists.

She acted without thinking. On automatic pilot, she was on her feet in front of John, blocking him from leaving the kitchen. "She's just a baby. She's crying. I'll take care of it."

"She's *crying?*" He stopped, the fierce look on his face falling away to concern. "I thought she was *dying*. Got trapped behind the dryer or something."

Alexandra took a step back, confused. He wasn't angry?

"Hailey, go check on her, would you?" John shook his head, relaxed, his hands slack. "That sounds like an air-raid siren. I thought we were under attack."

"It's amazing how something so small can make such a loud noise." Lame, Alexandra, real lame. But it was all she could think to say as the belated rush of adrenaline hit. There was no danger. John hadn't been angry. He'd been concerned.

As he was still.

Hailey raced away to check on the puppy. Within

seconds, the siren-pitched cry gave way to a yip of delight. "She's okay!"

"Good." John swiped a hand through his hair, standing those thick dark locks on end, before pinning Alexandra with his intense gaze. "You could have told us about the crying thing."

Was he still angry? "I figured you knew that babies cried."

"Yeah, but, well...is it going to happen again?"

"Probably." Alexandra felt an instinctive tightening in her stomach. Her chest felt hot and closed, making it hard to draw in air.

No, John wasn't angry. He was a powerful man, that was all. He'd been ready to help the puppy, not hurt her.

She'd been the one to read the situation wrong. To jump to the wrong conclusions. To assume a man who'd shown her nothing but kindness and generosity would also be capable of violent anger.

A part of her figured any man was. That was the truth, and she hated to admit it.

Remembering another man in her life, and his short-fused temper, she turned away, ashamed and confused and strangely blaming John for being a man, which made him like the others. And that wasn't fair.

"I don't suppose we can muzzle her?" John's eyes were flashing—he was teasing. Not at all angry.

Not every man became angry the way her father had. Or Patrick. The tightness inside her ebbed away and she could breathe deep again.

"I think you're going to have to buy earplugs," she was able to tease. "Or let Hailey keep the puppy with her."

"See? I knew it."

"Tomorrow I'll get a kennel at the pet store so we can train her. Don't worry—we'll put the kennel in Hailey's room."

"Good. I'm hungry. Let's dish up."

"Sure." She was still trembling with the aftereffects of an unnecessary fear. There was no danger. There never had been.

"Hey, are you okay?" His touch was sure and his words gentle. He stood before her, not just any man, but one of strength and goodness. Her very own hero.

How could anyone be so wonderful? So true?

She withdrew her hand and put distance between them. "I'm just hungry. Are you still afraid to try my cooking?"

"Shaking in my boots." John strode easily away in that powerful, athletic gait of his as if nothing were wrong, as if nothing had changed.

But something had.

Her hand tingled, warm and wonderful, where John had touched her. Even hours later when she was alone in the little bedroom in Bev's rental cottage, when she couldn't sleep. She sat up at the open window, remembering the heat of his touch, the connection of it, and watched a sickle moon rise into the starlit sky.

Chapter Nine

There was a creaking sound coming from the back of the house. The buzz of the tiny nine-inch television covered it up—almost. Alexandra's spine snapped straight. The sharp buzz of adrenaline fired into her veins and she flew off the edge of the couch.

There it was again. She didn't know where to run. Her feet were taking her into the bedroom. Even in the dark she could see the white curtain snap in the breeze of the open window. A window she'd left shut tight.

The darkness moved. The shadows became a man, and the faint gleam of metal became a gun aimed at her heart.

Patrick.

"You can't run, Alexandra. Didn't I tell you I'd hunt you down?"

She stumbled backward into the hallways, toward the light.

"You can't leave me, Alexandra. I need you." He stalked her, the shadows fading as he followed her into the living room, the brush of lamplight showing the hard anger in his black, unforgiving eyes.

There was nothing she could do to stop him. The front door was so far away. She couldn't run fast enough. She watched in horror as his finger squeezed the trigger—

She tore away, the scream dying in her throat....

There was only the sound of her ragged breath in the tiny room, where the distant floodlight from Bev's garage cast a friendly glow against the window, smeared with rain. The window was shut and locked.

She was alone and safe. It had been a dream. Nothing more.

Relief left her weak. She found the lamp by feel and turned it on. She followed the swath of light to the door, and into the tiny kitchen. The bulb above the sink was enough to work by—she filled a cup with water and popped it into the older-model microwave.

She hadn't dreamed of Patrick since the night she'd left. Cuddled up in the corner of her car, parked in the far end of a Wal-Mart parking lot in the shadow of a retired couple's mammoth motor home.

Although she wasn't visible from the road, she'd slept only a few hours—and fitfully. The fear felt in those dreams from that night remained real and blade-sharp as she rummaged in the drawer for the box of tea she'd brought with her.

Sweet peppermint scented the air as she ripped open the packet, unwinding the string from the bag and dunking the tea bag into her cup of hot water. The welcome aroma chased away some of the tightness inside her. But the fear remained.

It's all right. I'm safe here. She rescued her Bible from the tiny drop-leaf table in the corner and clutched it to her chest. She breathed in and out, slowing the fear, until there was only the sound of wind and rain.

There's no way Patrick can find me here. Not easily, anyway, and not tonight. It was a small town. Anyone could give him the information he needed—someone at the grocery store or someone on the street who went to the same church. Hers was the only rusty, faded old VW Bug around.

I should have headed to Minneapolis. Maybe Denver. Or back East, where the cities were gigantic and no one would remember another brown-haired woman among so many people.

The night's chill crept around her, and the damp

from the storm settled into her bones. She shivered. She felt alone. So very alone.

Lightning flashed through the night, a quick illumination of the cozy cottage, and then only darkness.

The electricity had gone out. As thunder pealed like rending sheet metal overhead, Alexandra stood from the chair. Halfway across the living room, another lightning bolt flashed, helping her find her way to bed.

She could only take each day step by step. Just like this. That was faith. That was life. She was not afraid.

Settling onto the bed, she found her tiny battery-operated reading light on the nightstand and turned it on. The small glow was enough to read by. But which passage?

She thumbed through the well-worn gold leafs until the page chose itself. The book of Jeremiah. There was nothing random about the passage that caught her eye. "For I know the plans I have for you," declares the Lord, "plans to prosper you and not to harm you, plans to give you hope and a future."

Faith. It was like groping blindly in the dark, but she trusted the way. Trusted the path beneath her feet.

Hope and a future. I could really use both right

now, Lord, she prayed. In the meantime, she was grateful to be staying with the Coreys. With John.

The thought of him was like a sweet wish. The tender longing for the weight of his bigger hand in hers.

She wasn't sure what to do about that. About John. Everything seemed so different. She closed her eyes but did not sleep.

"John." Alexandra skidded to a stop on the stone walkway in front of his house. "I thought you'd be gone by now."

"We're supposed to be. We're running late. It happens." He drank from a cup of coffee in one hand as he tugged a sprinkler into place with the other. "I've got a leak somewhere in the automatic system, so would you mind shutting this off in about twenty minutes?"

"I could be bribed into it. What's that you have there?"

"A fresh cup of coffee. I ground the beans myself. How about a cup?"

"It's a deal."

"Good." John bent to turn on the faucet. "It's warm this morning. Don't you think?"

A spray of cold water gently sprinkled her, and she shrieked, laughing, into the shelter of the covered porch. "You did that on purpose."

"Me? I'm too much of a gentleman. It was an accident."

"An accident, huh? I'm going to remember this. Expect retribution."

"The Bible bids us to never harm anyone."

"I suppose heaven always makes exceptions when a woman has a good case for revenge."

"Revenge of the sprinkler. I'm afraid."

"You should be." Laughing, with the wonderfully cool water evaporating on her bare arms, Alexandra followed him into the house. An ear-splitting yowl met her ears. "The puppy?"

"Every time Hailey gets out of her sight."

"You're in trouble, John."

"Don't I know it." He snared a cup and filled it. "Since you're here, maybe you could watch over her while we're gone. She doesn't like to be alone."

"It's a good thing you're so strict, or that puppy would be in danger of becoming spoiled."

"Now you're making fun of me. I'm a tough guy. I don't take any nonsense. I run a tight ship. Everyone lives in fear of me."

"I've noticed. You're as tough as a marshmallow. I bet the puppy slept in Hailey's arms last night."

"I'd never allow such a thing." He winked. "I couldn't talk Hailey out of it, but there's an upside. The puppy stopped that high-decibel wailing."

"How's the training going?"

"Accidents abound." He held out the cup to her. "We survived, though. You could have an interesting morning."

"I'll see what I can teach her." She accepted the mug, and her fingers bumped his. Heat zinged up her arm.

I refuse to be attracted to him. There. Alexandra turned away as if the collision of their fingertips meant nothing to her and went in search of the sugar. She found it in the pantry. When she turned around, John had left the room. The faint rumbling of his deep voice could be heard from upstairs.

He had a wonderful tone, masculine and strong without being overbearing. The warmth in his murmured words, the caring she heard as he spoke with his daughter, made her heart twist hard.

Not knowing what to do, she gazed into the depths of the serviceable stoneware mug that fit so wonderfully into both hands. The coffee warmed her palms and seeped into her soul. She stared at the dark liquid, wishing. Just wishing.

If she ran, she'd be safe. From the past, from heartbreak, from finding out that her mother was right. That was the real reason she'd let things go so far with Patrick.

She willed away the past with all the strength of her being, but there it was, a boomerang spinning back around for her to catch, gaining speed with its descent. She couldn't stop it. Not even the bold taste of hot coffee could soothe it away.

She heard the same words she had heard as a little girl, then as an adolescent, then a teenager, over and over again, as her mother had slurred them. *Don't think you'll grow up to be no different from me, Alexandra. Men don't have hearts. No hearts. You remember that. If a man says he loves you, then you know he's lyin'. Who's gonna love you?*

The one time Alexandra had dared to hope that some man could really love her, a good and decent man, she'd been wrong. So very wrong.

Cradling the cup in both hands, she breathed in the comforting scent of steaming coffee. Let the boiling hot brew burn down her throat, but still the feelings and the past remained.

"Alexandra!" Hailey appeared on the stairs, carefully cradling a little black bundle in both arms. "You're here! You're here! I'm real glad, too, 'cuz she cries like a baby every time I leave her alone." She bumped noses with her puppy and her voice changed, higher, sweeter. "Yes, you do, don't you, little baby?"

"Have you found a name for her yet?"

"Nope. I sorta like Emma, but I don't know yet." Hailey stopped moving, so that Alexandra could pet the puppy. "She doesn't like to be all alone, so I'm awful glad you're here."

"Me, too." The puppy was warm and content, and wiggled in delight as Alexandra stroked one furry ear. "I'll take good care of her for you."

"I know." As if there were never a doubt, as if Hailey had never had a real worry, she handed over the puppy with a kiss to its silky head.

Safe and beloved, the puppy buried its warm nose in the crook of Alexandra's arm and whimpered as Hailey bid it goodbye.

John came racing down the stairs, a duffel bag swinging over his shoulder. "I left a note on the counter with the credit card."

"For the pet store. Right." Alexandra could barely think as he swept by, reached out to pat the puppy's paw. John's fingers brushed over Alexandra's bare forearm. The faintest of touches. It could have been warm air whispering over her skin, but it was him. His touch. His heat. His presence burning through her.

"Have a great day," he called out, already striding away, the athletic bag slung over one broad shoulder, his muscled legs stretching out to carry him from her sight.

The front door opened, then closed, and she was alone. Strangely missing him.

She *really* didn't feel attracted to him. Really. John Corey was like a white knight of old, the greatest of warriors and the noblest of men. What maiden wouldn't gaze upon him with admiration? That's all this feeling was.

He was her employer. It was as simple as that. He paid her to clean his house. Their relationship wasn't personal. In fact, they didn't have a *relationship*—they weren't even friends.

Remember Patrick? And the dream she had last night? Wasn't that all the indication she needed? Worry about what's right in front of you, Alexandra. Doing a good job for the Coreys. Keeping safe. Seizing this chance to put a little bit more cash in her wallet. Her thin stack of twenties had already dwindled alarmingly.

The sound of tires crunching on the gravel driveway brought her to the front window. Was it John? Had he forgotten something? Or Bev coming over to use the guest shower—the electricity on the other side of the ranch was still out from the storm.

It was a police cruiser, polished and gleaming in the cheerful morning sun. The uniformed man inside climbed out slowly, looking around. He caught sight of her in the window and tipped his hat with a friendly smile. Alexandra opened the door.

"Miss Sims? John told me to come talk to you. Says you have a problem I can help you with."

"I'm not sure what you can do. Please, come in."

"I'd rather stay out here on the porch, if you don't mind. Spend a lot of my day sittin'." He swept off his hat, ambling into the shade. "I know you're probably skittish, considerin' all you've been through, but you're not the first woman on this earth to be afraid of someone. It's important to know you're not alone in this. Between me and John, we'll do our best to keep you safe."

The sincerity of his pledge felt like the sweetest of blessings.

Taking a seat on the swing on John's front porch, with the puppy warm and snug in her arms, Alexandra told the officer about the charming man she'd fallen in love with. He'd seemed so kind to her, so perfect.

Just like John.

The bell above the shop's door clattered, and from the back room John didn't look up from the thick parts book. "Be right with you," he called out.

"You in the back?" Cameron, the town's only lawman, didn't let the Employees Only sign stop him. "This morning I got time to talk to that young woman out at your place."

"Thanks for taking the time." John found the part number, scribbled it down on the back of a packing slip and slammed the book shut.

"No problem. It's hard to tell. These things can go either way. She may never have a lick of trouble from that fella. Or he could show up here tomorrow.'' The sheriff helped himself to the old refrigerator in the back corner and hauled out a bottle of iced tea. ''She gave me a good description, and if he drives down the main street of this town, I'll spot him.''

''Good. Thanks, Cameron. You're a good man.''

''I owe ya one.'' Cam held up the bottle in a salute. ''Staying in your mom's extra cottage ought to help out. She'll be hard to find. No phone bill. No utilities. Plus, I'm bettin' you don't mind watchin' over her. She's downright pretty.''

''I can see where you're going with this.'' Old friends from high school, Cam wasn't fooling John one bit. ''She's pretty, but she needs protecting. Not the town cop playing matchmaker for her.''

''Hey, you're awful defensive. Maybe you noticed she's pretty, too.''

''She's working for me, that's all. Don't go reading something into nothing.'' John felt his face heat up a few degrees. ''She's in a lot of trouble. I want to help her. That's it. That's all. End of story.''

''Sure it is. Anyone with eyes can see that. Hey, don't get so bent out of shape. I've known you a long time, John. I know how hard you took Bobbie's death. I'm not saying you shouldn't grieve, but it's been too long. Maybe you oughta think about that.''

''Don't need to.'' Not even Cam understood.

''I've got civic duties to perform. Laws to uphold, and all that.'' Cam headed for the door.

The bell jangled, and he was alone. Alone with a knotted-up stomach and this strange horrible feeling right smack-dab in the center of his chest.

Cameron was wrong. John didn't feel anything for Alexandra. It wasn't like that.

He couldn't afford to feel too much at all.

Holding down the guilt, shutting off his emotions, he crossed the alley to the warehouse and went in search of a U-joint. It was tough to find the part. He really had to search since his mind was on Alexandra.

She sure could stir him up. Maybe because she needed him and his protection, and that made him feel worthy for the first time in a long while. Since Bobbie was alive.

His knuckles collided with the hard plane of the wood door, sending sharp streaks of pain into the bones. He'd missed the doorknob entirely—probably because he couldn't see.

Thinking of Bobbie and how he failed her could bring him to his knees. Steal the vision from his eyes. The warmth from his soul. *Inadequate* wasn't the word. Neither was *failure*. He could see it over and over again—her glove slipping, feeling the leather stretch to the breaking point, knowing that she was going to fall three thousand feet down the face of the mountainside.

Lord, I failed her. You put her into my care, and I messed up. More than anyone ever could. I failed. His forehead smacked against the door, something solid to cling to when it felt as if God wasn't answering.

John knew one thing for certain—for whatever reason, God had guided Alexandra to him and the shelter of his family. For as long as she needed it, he would be there.

This time he would not fail.

"Where is that granddaughter of mine?" Bev whipped off her glasses with her free hand as she marched up the path to the back deck. "I swear, summer came early and with a vengeance. Whew, is it hot. I'm going to put this in the refrigerator and help myself to some tea."

"Let me get that for you." Alexandra clipped the safety catch on the pruning shears she'd found in a dusty corner of the outside shed. "And since I'm going in that direction, hand over the sack, too. I'll take it in."

"What a dear you are. There are a few leftovers from my Ladies' Aid meeting. We had a potluck. Hmm, it was good." Bev gladly relinquished the heavy grocery bag. "How's the puppy working out?"

"Terrible. It was such a mistake." Alexandra bit her lip when Hailey's shriek of delight and a puppy's happy yip sounded on the other side of the house.

"So I see." Bev dropped her purse on the table, eyeing the tall, overgrown bushes alongside part of the deck with obvious speculation. "Glad to see someone's finally dealing with those roses. They're beautiful, and John can't keep up with them."

"Just doing what I can while I'm here." Alexandra peeked into the sack and spotted several plastic containers. "This is enough for a couple of meals."

"Thought you could use some help. Hailey is a handful." Sparkling with grandmotherly love, Bev caught sight of her granddaughter. "Oh, excuse me. I've got to hug my girl."

"Sure." Alexandra's throat ached as she stepped away. There was something that hurt inside her as she saw Bev hurry down the steps and across the grass, arms held wide.

"Grammy!" Hailey sparkled like the brightest star in the heavens as she ran, tumbling into her grandmother's arms. "Alexandra and me, we went shoppin' for my puppy. And we got to take her right into the store and everything!"

"Is that right? Let's see this puppy of yours."
Bev took Hailey's hand, turning toward the little
black dog bounding through the grass toward them.

More than anything, Alexandra wanted a life like
this. With all that she was, all that she would be,
she wanted to step into a world like this. Be a part
of a family this openly affectionate and accepting.
Where love—and spirits—flourished.

Bev knelt to meet her new grandpuppy, her happy
chuckle of delight blending with Hailey's as the dog
leaped and licked and wiggled. This was such a safe
place, but it felt like a fairy tale. Something Alexandra had read about, and she was glad the heroine
in the story found true happiness and love. But after
Alexandra closed the book, she was still in her own
world. Alone. Not at all sure if she could find the
same joy or if she deserved it.

Remember the verse from Jeremiah? She had
hope and a future. She had to cling to that. To believe good things were possible.

But the past clung to her like a shadow. Her
mother's words and Patrick's polite, very gradual
control. Odd how he'd often said the same thing to
her, how lucky she was that he'd fallen in love with
her. In all her twenty-four years, no one else had.
Don't think about the past, Alexandra. Or those
harsh, painful words Patrick had said to her. The

ones that made her feel smaller, less worthy, less everything.

But here, she felt different. Renewed. The bright cheerful sounds of Hailey's laughter flitted on the wind into the kitchen. Bev's genteel alto voice answered, and the puppy yipped, bringing her back to the present.

"Hey." A man's voice startled her. "Come in. Earth to Alexandra."

"John." She almost dropped the plastic glass she was holding.

There he was, too handsome to look at, even in a simple blue striped seersucker shirt, tucked into comfortable-looking, wash-worn jeans. The sight of him took her breath away. Made her wonder what it would be like to let those rock-solid arms fold around her. Made her wish she had the chance to know the feel of his comfort, his strength and his heartbeat against her cheek.

"Want a glass of iced tea?" It was all she could think of to say, which was better than blurting out what she was really thinking—now there's a good-looking man.

"Sure, but you don't have to wait on me. Here, let me help." He took the glass, his big callused fingers closing over hers, leaving her breathless and trembling and feeling so incredibly female against his masculine strength. He towered over her as he used the ice maker in the refrigerator door. "Did Hailey make you max out my card at the pet store?"

"We did our best." Taking Hailey to the pet store was another memory she'd tucked into her heart. They were three females on the loose—including the puppy—going up and down the aisles searching for everything they wanted, and a lot of stuff they didn't need. "Hailey is a serious shopper. When she gets to be a teenager, watch out."

"Don't I know it? Mom has taught Hailey everything she knows. Which is, the more the merrier, and you can't have enough shoes."

"At least Bev's trained her right."

John filled a third glass and didn't move aside when Alexandra sidled up to him to open the refrigerator door. They were so close, all she would have to do was reach out and her hand would brush his arm. She would feel that connection, that unique, strengthening power that made her heart soar.

Unaware, John slid the last glass on the counter. "Let me." He reached in front of her, his arm muscled and rock-hard, brushing against her forearm as he lifted the pitcher right out of her hands. "I heard Cameron came out to see you today. Did he treat you right?"

"He sure did." It was impossible not to notice the caring in his voice. "Cameron promised he'd watch the traffic coming through town for me."

"It's a small town. It wouldn't be too hard to spot a stranger matching Patrick's description. We're here if you need us."

"You're going beyond the call of duty to help me. I don't know why, but I appreciate it. I really do."

"What's the mystery? You need help, and we're helping you." John said the words lightly. He pushed his feelings deeper inside where he couldn't feel them and didn't need to wonder what they meant. Didn't need to admit he admired her more with every day that passed. Admired her? Well, it was more than that.

Alexandra stood off to the side with her arms wrapped around her middle, looking so alone. Her chin was up, her spine stiff. She looked ready for a fight. Ready to stand up for herself. Such a frail woman, petite and wispy and as lean as a willow, but there was strength in her. He could see it.

Whatever hardship she was running from, she would recover. She'd come back from it. He *knew* it, down deep. Maybe here could be a resting place for her. He liked knowing that he'd helped to make that possible. That he'd made a difference for her.

She could stay here all summer. No reason why she couldn't. She could watch Hailey full-time and ferry her around to her hundred thousand lessons and social appointments. And then, every evening

when he came home from work, he'd have the
chance to see her. She was so beautiful and alone
and vulnerable, and when he looked at her he saw
a future for the first time—

Whoa. Hold on, John. You can't go thinking like
that. Pain arrowed through him, deep enough to rock
his soul. He thought of Bobbie, laid to rest in the
town cemetery and the day he'd buried her in a
white coffin. Of three days before when he'd held
her lifeless hand in the helicopter, while his friends
did everything they could to try and keep her heart
beating, to give her the chance at life.

And failed. How the flat line went forever on the
monitor, and the nurse put her face in her hands and
wept. Everyone said it wasn't his fault. He'd done
everything he could to save her.

No one knew that when she'd been falling to her
death, she'd locked her gaze on his. Not looking
down, but up at him. She'd always looked up to him,
always told him he was her very own hero come to
life.

Hero? He'd been the worst failure. The worst sort
of man that day, who hadn't been strong enough.

He didn't know if he was any stronger now. "I
hope you're not getting tired of us already. I told
you it was tough being around us. It was Hailey,
wasn't it? She wore you out shopping. Made you

afraid to hang around and spend the summer with her.''

"That was it. Shopping with Hailey and her puppy was the toughest job I've ever had. No one should be made to work under such conditions. Laughter. Giggling. The puppy to snuggle. Ice cream afterward.''

"Torture by chocolate. It happens. I get too much of it here. There ought to be a law against that kind of abuse. A person can only take so much fudge sauce.''

"Exactly. I'm going to report you to your cop friend. Tell him about the laughter in this house.''

"Scandalous. The neighbors complain.''

"The neighbors are a couple of miles away.''

"Yep. With the wild social life I lead, the noise carries a far distance.''

"Right. Hailey says you only date the TV.''

"My affection for baseball is only surpassed by my obsession with football, but I'm not ashamed to admit it.''

"That's the first step toward recovery.'' Alexandra snatched two of the glasses, leaving him one.

"You don't approve of sports?''

"Sure, I love them. I'm not sure I approve of sitting on the couch instead of being outside where you can actually participate in a sport.''

"You think I'm a couch potato, is that it?''

"You sure look like one to me." He looked about as soft as a hunk of steel, but she didn't need to tell him that. "A serious couch potato. One that's growing roots right into the sofa cushion."

"Yeah? I suppose it takes one to know one."

"What does that mean?" She waited while he opened the screen door. "You think I look like a couch potato?"

"If the sofa fits…"

"I'll have you know I have plenty of outdoor activities. I hike."

"No kidding?" All at once the shutters were down, as John led the way onto the deck. There was a spring to his step, a liveliness that made the shadows in his eyes fade away, like morning mist giving way to the sun. "Me, too.

"The guide I gave you ought to lead you to some great trails in this part of Montana, not just at Yellowstone. But since you're not hanging around, I guess you'll just have to suffer without seeing some of the best backcountry you'll probably see."

"You're trying to tempt me with promises of great natural beauty."

"Sure. It takes a hiker to know one. The question is, can you resist?" John set his glass on the wrought-iron table in the umbrella's shade. "Hailey and I always take a trip when school lets out. We head up into the backcountry and spend the night. Why don't you come with us?''

"You really know how to tempt a girl."

"Then you'd be interested?"

"If the terms were right." She flashed him one of her pretty smiles as she swished away.

Marriage is like this. John wished the thought away, but it remained, steady like a light always burning and as sure as a new day dawning. He'd missed the companionship, the talk and the ease of being with another person who accepted you.

Except this wasn't a marriage; this was only reminding him of that amazing time in his life. That once-in-a-lifetime place, and he had no business confusing Alexandra's friendship with his longing for a wife. To be married again. To have a woman at his side.

Alexandra made him think about what he could never have again. That's what this hard, sharp feeling was in his chest. The longing for a wife one day—the one thing he could never deserve.

It had nothing to do with Alexandra. That's why he couldn't look anywhere else as she gazed up at him with those deep luminous eyes. Why he felt entranced when the breeze caressed a lock of her silken hair against the soft curve of her face. She looked a little better tonight, more relaxed. More assured.

He liked seeing that change in her.

"I'll be right back." Her numerous silver rings flashed in the sunlight, drawing his attention to those slim hands of hers, so delicate and feminine, so graceful even doing something ordinary like holding a plastic glass full of iced tea.

Beautiful hands. She was beautiful in every way, and it ensnared his heart and broke it all at the same time.

You can't have her, John. And if she knew what you'd done, she wouldn't want you. He squeezed his eyes shut, blocking out the sight of her walking away from him, but he already knew how she walked. He could see it in his mind's eye. The curled ends of her brown hair swaying with her gait. The quiet way she moved, like a morning breeze in an alpine meadow. The way she gave a little flick of her wrist when she reached for the handrail. Her sneakers padded down the steps, and the bottom stair squeaked when she stepped on it.

You're in love with her, John. The single truth ran through his mind like the clear chime of a church bell, leaving no doubt. He wanted to deny it. He wanted to be noble and say there was no way he'd allow himself to feel that way—he had no right, it was not possible, it was only longing and loneliness and anything else he could think of.

But there was no excuse on earth that could

change the sharp pain that expanded with every beat of his heart. He loved Alexandra. The way a man loved a woman he wants to marry—truly and deeply.

He felt as if the sun had gone out. The brightness dimmed from the day, and the shadows crept through him with the cold fingers of a winter's night. He felt trapped in a cold dark place he couldn't climb out of, and he watched, as if at a great distance, as Alexandra breezed across the lush green lawn, her voice a dulcet tone that touched his soul.

He couldn't hear what she was saying. She handed the glass to Bev, with that gentle quiet smile that made his soul ache with a longing so intense, he'd didn't know which way was up or down.

He loved Alexandra. It coursed through him like a raging river in a time of flood. Like blinding sunlight glaring off a mountain glacier that had been icing over and thawing, icing and thawing for a thousand years. Like a violent clap of thunder overhead that was the only sound in the world for that one brief instant, so loud and frightening and overwhelming, it made the ground shake.

I can't feel this way. John wanted to pray for this staggering emotion to lift from his heart, never to return. He felt choked and suffocated all at once, holding back the bright hot flood of love from taking over his soul.

He could never let anyone know that he loved her. Especially Alexandra. So angelic and perfect and unbelievable. Look how she smiled. When her smile reached her eyes, and made them shine with light, he could see heaven.

He felt unworthy to the core. To his soul. He could not move, paralyzed on the spot, as Alexandra knelt to pat the puppy's soft head. Every movement she made was gentle and loving—how she ruffled her fingertips through the pup's soft black fur, the tone of her voice and the way she laughed so wonderfully with Hailey when the little girl bent close.

I don't deserve to love Alexandra. She deserves better.

It was tough, burying the feelings deep, but he did. He had no right to her. He couldn't stop the powerful tides of his heart as he watched her steal the extra bubble wand from Hailey's outstretched hand and kept it high as the puppy leaped. Her soft laughter filled his life and his heart like spring did the breeze, like dawn changed the world, and he was changed.

He dared to look long enough to see Alexandra sweep the soapy wand along the ground, creating giant bubbles for the puppy to chase.

"Look, Daddy! She can sure jump high!" Hailey gleefully swiped her wand, too. More iridescent bubbles rose from the ground, lifting into the air.

"Did you see that? She can jump as high as an angel."

"Look." Alexandra made more bubbles with the elegant sweep of her slim arm. The puppy leaped into the center of the big bubble, popping it, but for an instant the iridescence enveloped her.

"Angel wings." Alexandra formed another long bubble, and the pup leaped into the center of it again.

"Cool! I know! I know!" Hailey's joy filled the air like heaven's touch. "I'm gonna name her Angel."

"Perfect," Alexandra praised. "A girl can never have too many guardian angels."

"That's right," Bev agreed.

John had never felt so bleak, so disconnected from life, even though he forced his feet forward, pretending nothing was wrong. Pretending he didn't want to draw Alexandra into his arms, hold her against his chest and never let go.

Chapter Ten

With the warmth of the evening still lifting her spirits and the temperate breeze whipping through the open windows of her Bug, Alexandra struggled not to think of John.

Impossible.

They had a connection. She felt it when they touched. When they talked. When he made her laugh. No man had ever made her feel this way. She was afraid no man ever would.

John wasn't going to marry again. He wasn't going to fall in love with her. She knew that. Was she even ready to love someone new, after Patrick? How did she stop her feelings?

John probably had no clue she felt this way about him. He was simply a kind man and a Good Samaritan. It wasn't as if she could ever let him know how she felt. Right?

She rounded the last bumping corner of the gravel driveway and saw the strange car parked in front of the little yellow cottage tucked in a stand of cotton-woods. With the thick evening shadows, she couldn't see what kind of car it was. Except that she didn't recognize it as belonging to any of the Cor-eys.

Patrick. She stomped on the brakes, the wheels locked up and the tires skidded in the gravel. Dust flew around her as she sat with her fingers gripping the steering wheel so tight, they ached. Her pulse thudded in her throat as she sat stock-still in the road, in plain sight of the house. It was too late to turn around. He would already have seen her.

What do I do, Lord? She took a deep breath, ready to shift into reverse. Wait. Those were Mon-tana plates. A woman stepped out of the shadows, someone about her age, wearing a pair of jeans and a grass-green sweater with a big fish on it. Her smile was friendly and she looked familiar. Oh, Alexandra had seen her in church. She'd been sitting on the pew in front of them.

She looked nice, too, like she'd be a good friend. Hopeful, Alexandra climbed out of her car. "Hi."

"Hi, I'm Kirby McKaslin." She pushed a lock of hair behind her ear, as if she were a little nervous.

"I didn't know if you'd be interested, but a bunch of us meet for Bible Study every Tuesday night at the town coffee shop. Would you like to join us?"

"Yes." An evening of fellowship was something she'd needed desperately. "The coffee shop in town? The one on the corner?"

"That's the one. If you want, you can ride with me. We can go together."

"Great. Let me get my Bible." Heaven was smiling on her today, Alexandra thought, as she raced inside. She felt like she used to, before Patrick, when she was free to do anything she wanted without worrying how he would react. What he would think.

She didn't have to look over her shoulder as she locked the house up tight and followed Kirby to her car.

Later that night, as she finished her prayers and crawled beneath the quilt Bev had dug out of her hall linen closet, and between the softest sheets she'd ever known, Alexandra gave thanks for the best day she'd had in years.

When she woke up with the first rays of the sun smiling through the crack in the curtains, she remembered the verse from Jeremiah. Good things *were* happening to her. Hope began seeping into her heart again, warm and substantial.

She had to deal with this *thing* she felt for John. This infatuation, for the lack of a better word. A crush. She had to recognize it for what it was. It was all one-sided. Anything coming of it was impossible. She needed to concentrate on the problems she already had. She didn't need to go searching for more problems by mistaking kindness for romance—besides, John wasn't interested in marrying a second time.

After she'd showered and dressed for the day, Alexandra grabbed her devotional and her Bible from the nightstand. The kitchen was dim, and she pulled the curtains open. What a view.

She'd been here long enough, quietly in one place. If Patrick were following her, he'd have caught up with her by now. The tension coiled inside her began to unwind as she sipped her cup of coffee and gazed out the small window at such a great, beautiful world.

When she opened her devotional to the marked page, she had to marvel at how many times she found the passage she most needed to see—when she needed to see it. *I am leaving you with a gift— peace of mind and heart. And the peace I give isn't like the peace the world gives. So don't be troubled or afraid.*

She felt stronger. Better.

Peace touched her, not only from the beautiful mountains jutting ruggedly toward the crystal-blue sky and the rolling green meadows in every direction. But from within. She let peace fill up the wounded places within her heart, like light chasing away the shadows, making her whole.

Alexandra opened the window and breathed in the morning air, letting the warm wind touch her face. This is where she was meant to be. Right here. Right now. She could feel it down deep.

The sound of a pickup's engine cut through the serenity of the morning. She figured it was probably Gerald, driving along the main driveway from the farmhouse. When she spotted a bright red truck, she was surprised.

John.

What was he doing? John couldn't begin to explain it as he cut the engine. The little rental house, which had long been the hired man's house, before the harvesting was hired out, had seen better days, but it had never looked quite so charming as he gazed on it now. That had to do with the woman standing in the threshold, the sunlight streaking auburn highlights into her silken hair that framed her heart-shaped face—the face of the woman he loved.

You're in big trouble, John, if you let your feelings get the best of you. He took a steadying breath and hopped out of the truck.

She was coming toward him in slow steps across the porch, hesitant and demure. The light blue denim shorts and dark blue T-shirt made her look like something in a fashion magazine. With her bare feet, she looked so casually beautiful he couldn't make his brain function well enough to figure out what to say.

"This is a surprise." She leaned one slim shoulder against the support post.

The first thing he noticed was that her smile shone in her eyes, bright and true and more amazing than anything he'd ever seen. She made him feel more everything than he'd ever felt. Suddenly he was aware he was slouching a little bit, so he stood up a little straighter. And his hair was tumbling into his eyes—he'd better remember to get a haircut.

Hold on, John. It's not like you're going to start dating her. What you feel is one thing, but there's only one outcome here. She can never be mine.

"I know it's early, I don't mean to interrupt. I just dropped Hailey off at the bus stop. Figured I might as well bring you this, since I had it. Thought you could use it."

"Oh?"

Good thing she didn't look at him like a woman captivated. She seemed friendly enough, but not coy, not interested in him. That made it easier to hand her the small bag as if it wasn't a big deal.

It wasn't, really. He was simply doing his best to protect her.

He liked the way she lit up when she looked inside the bag. It made him feel good, as if he'd done the right thing.

"A cell phone."

"Figured you didn't want to be stranded out here without a way to call for help. Not that you'll need it. But just in case."

"That was thoughtful of you, John."

"Had an extra one sitting around." That was almost the truth, he thought guiltily, as he moved close. So close, the apple scent of her shampoo tickled his nose. He could see the flecks of black in her brown eyes. He could sense the warmth of her spirit, of her soul, as if it were a match to his.

He jerked back as if burned. Creating distance. Putting enough space between them. Still, he could feel her, as if their hearts beat together. From five feet away.

What was he going to do?

Anguished, he walked away, calling over his shoulder in a strained voice he hoped sounded normal enough. "I'll be late tonight. Got some volunteer stuff in town. Just go ahead and drop Hailey off at Mom's."

"No problem." Her smile was pure sunshine and genuine appreciation. "Thanks again, John."

"Hey, no problem."

The way she said his name twisted him up inside.

Her dulcet voice, her warmhearted tone… No, he couldn't do this anymore. He marched across the gravel to his truck, yanking open the door blindly and landing on the seat, breathing as hard as if he'd climbed Pike's Peak.

She lifted her free hand, waving in her dainty, female sort of way, a beautiful, just-right way that made him hurt even more.

He put his truck in gear and raced away, churning gravel and dust in his wake, but he didn't care. He had to get out of there. Away from her. The image of her grew smaller and smaller in the rearview mirror, a lone woman standing on a crooked porch, watching him go.

Something had gone wrong. She didn't know what it was, not exactly, she thought as she wrung out the mop. Soap bubbles popped in the air as she lowered the mop to the floor. She swished hard, breathing heavy, intending to wash this floor better than any housecleaner before her ever had, but little Angel leaped into the way, growling in play.

John had turned away so abruptly this morning. Was it because of something she did? How could it be? There could be only one logical explanation— he'd stepped so close to her she could feel the heat from his arm on hers. They'd almost been touching.

So close she could smell the spicy aftershave cling-ing to him, and the fabric softener on his shirt.

Her stomach had flip-flopped strangely and for one moment she'd turned to look at him, at the shaved-smooth cut of his strong jaw and his rugged profile.

What would it be like to have reached out and laid her hand on his arm? Would he feel as hard and substantial as he looked? And what was wrong with her anyway that she kept thinking of these things?

She'd like to explain it away, but she couldn't. The plain truth was that her attraction for John Corey wasn't fading away. It was growing stronger every time she saw him.

Just stop thinking about him. You're just looking for a hero, Alexandra. Someone to save you. From the pain of your childhood. From the heartache of being without a family. From the devastation of fall-ing in love with the wrong man. She'd tried to give those things up to the Lord and look to heaven for that level of deep healing.

But faith was sometimes a difficult thing. It was hard to trust in the Father's great love, when she'd never known real love before. She clung to her faith with all she had, but some days it was harder. The Lord works in His own time. She would have to be patient, that was all.

When the time was right, she would fall in love.

The Lord would lead her to the right man, one who was kind. Whose love was true. Right?

One thing she knew for sure—that man wouldn't be John Corey.

Did she embarrass herself this morning? Maybe. Did he guess that she was interested in him?

Great. How was she going to look him in the eye again?

Refusing to think about *that,* she went back to work.

"John, you awake?"

Something knocked into his elbow—his friend's fist. That brought John back to the present. "Yeah, sure. I'm wide-awake."

"Didn't look like it to me." Zach Drake had been his friend since kindergarten and winked at him, whispering so he wouldn't distract from the county sheriff giving a talk at the front of the meeting room. "Know what I think? I bet you were daydreaming. You've got a woman on your mind."

"What I have is indigestion. Ate too much chili over at the diner."

"Sure. You just keep telling yourself that. Maybe you'll believe it." Zach didn't take his gaze from the stern-looking man who was now waving a pointer at a chart. "That's a real nice woman you've hired to take care of things at your place. She wouldn't have anything to do with your mood.''

"Of course not." John lied flat-out.

"Hmm." As if he knew far too much, being a newlywed himself, Zach winked again.

John's jaw tightened so hard, his teeth clacked together. "How did you know about Alexandra?"

"She went to the coffee shop last night. Word gets around in a small town."

Great. Just what he needed. Everyone meant well, sure, but before long Zach wouldn't be the only one commenting on how pretty Alexandra was. Or how long he'd been a lonely widower. Not that he cared. Nope, he could take it—well, he thought he could. But if Alexandra was the topic of the local gossip, then it wouldn't be as hard for that Patrick fellow to track her down.

He was concerned about her, is all. It was his duty. He took responsibility seriously.

"Isn't that her?" Zach gestured toward the only window in the room. The one that faced the alley way where an old yellow VW was turning into a potholed parking lot.

That was sure Alexandra's car. John sat up straight, straining to watch as she pulled up in front of a run-down place, where a faded sign from what had to be the fifties proclaimed The Wash Tub.

Sure enough, she climbed out, car keys dangling

from one hand as she pushed the seat forward and wrestled two bulging pillowcases from the back. Why didn't he think to offer her the use of his washer and dryer?

Too late now. Every one would notice if he sprinted for the door to catch her. Like Zach, would they all be thinking he was in love with Alexandra? That was no one's business but his own. His conscience bit him good as he watched her saunter up to the double glass doors.

She stopped to redistribute her load. The bags didn't look heavy, just bulky. And it was all he could do not to leap out of his seat and help her. She managed okay, and smiled at a woman exiting the Laundromat with a child on her hip. What a smile. John figured a man could look on that smile for the rest of his life and never tire of it.

And even his guilt wasn't strong enough to chase away the love he felt when she slipped through the doors and out of his sight. Leaving a yearning for the sight of her sweetness and her goodness that did not fade.

Alexandra pushed in the money slot and hit the start button. The dryer hummed to life, squeaking a little as the big drum started to turn, tossing her sheets and towels into a colorful whirl. She'd done a quick load earlier in the week so she had towels, but she was wearing the last of her clean clothes. Good thing the Laundromat wasn't busy. She could use three of the four machines.

Digging into her jeans pocket for more quarters, she didn't bother to turn around when the door opened. Looked like she spoke too soon—now there would be a sudden rush for the washing machines, knowing her luck. Well, maybe she'd only use two of the machines, since that would be polite.

"Hey, stranger." John set two disposable cups and a white paper sack on the lid of the washing machine beside her. "I come bearing gifts."

"Again? Hey, I like this." Okay, so she'd add *generous* to the list of John's admirable qualities. "Are those cookies from the coffee shop?"

"Yep. Being the stellar guy I am, I'm even going to share these double-chocolate-chip-fudge cookies with you. For a price."

"I knew there was a catch. Some things are too good to be true."

"Exactly." He popped the top off of one cup. "Do you want peppermint or apple cinnamon?"

"Peppermint." She took the cup he offered. "My favorite. What's the catch? They say nothing is ever really free."

"You're a wise woman, Alexandra. For a cookie and this cup of tea, I'm going to ask you to use my washer and dryer next time you need to. I'm not about to let you go to this kind of trouble.''

"This is no trouble. I'm used to Laundromats. I have a book, see?'' She gestured to a paperback facedown on top of the dryer. "Besides, how can I use your machines? That would be taking advantage of you.''

"The way I see it, we're taking advantage of you.''

"How exactly are you doing that? You're giving me shelter and a job. You're watching over me, in case I run into trouble. And you've let me become a part of your family, just for a little while. I owe you.''

"Guess it's a matter of perspective. See, I owe you because my floors shine when I walk in the door, and the towels smell really good and they're all clean and folded up on the shelves. And my TV screen has never been so dust free.''

"That's why you're paying me.''

"Wait. There's more. Hailey is happier with you in our house. Her puppy is housebroken because you took the time to teach her. Hailey told me you agreed to bake cupcakes for the school party next week.''

"In a moment of weakness, I said yes. Actually, I've discovered I can't say no to her.''

"A common malady when it comes to Hailey. I have the same problem myself."

"I didn't notice a bit."

That made him chuckle, and a dimple dug into his cheeks. A smile that made him open wide, and she could see the heart of him. Struggling to always do right, fearing he always fell short. Vulnerable and strong, and all too human. A man who brought tea and cookies to a woman who'd been down on her luck.

He'd never hurt her. Or anyone. She realized it in a heartbeat, as if heaven had whispered in her ear. Deep inside, where it mattered, behind the dependable father and Good Samaritan and the faithful son and the loyal friend, John Corey was a trustworthy man. Down to his soul.

Paper rustled as he held the bag open for her. "Try one. There's no heaven on earth, but this is about as close to it as anyone can get."

"That good, huh?" She took a bite and sighed as her taste buds detected the rich fudge and real chocolate chips.

"Thought you'd like it." He seemed pleased as he tossed the drained tea bag into the air. It made a perfect arc into the nearby garbage can. "Can you beat that?"

"You look awfully confident. You don't think I can."

"Nope. I was all-state in high school."

"Really? So was I. I was a starter on the girls' varsity." She wound up and sent the bag spinning into the can. "Two points."

"Here. Let's go two for two." He crumbled a napkin and aimed and missed. "Aw. I can't believe it."

"Some of us have it. Some of us don't." She sent a napkin in a perfect arc and it made the metal garbage can ring when it hit. "I guess that extra cookie belongs to me."

"If I would have won, I'd share."

"Sure, go ahead and make me feel bad. I'm a chocolate-cookie hog."

"Hey, I didn't want to say anything because I didn't want to hurt your feelings, but it's a real problem. One I'd sure be happy to help you with. Maybe it'd be best to give me the whole cookie—"

"Here's half, mister, and be grateful." She broke the soft cookie in two pieces and held out the larger one for him.

His fingers brushed hers and there it was, the connection she'd felt before. Like grabbing hold of a high-voltage line. There was no mistaking the power of it.

"After Hailey's last day of school, we always head up into the backcountry for an old-fashioned camp-out. We hike, we bird-watch. We get all the nature we can stand and then we come home where there's running water. Electricity. My sports channel.''

"I bet you two have a great time, but I'll miss Hailey." And you. "This works out great. I've been wanting some time to go clothes shopping—"

"No, that's not what I meant." What was he doing? A sane man wouldn't do this, but the words tumbled out of his mouth anyway and he couldn't stop them. Maybe he didn't want to. "I want you to come with us.''

"Camping? You and me? Alone?"

"Hailey will come, too. You'll be as safe as a kitten, and I'll be a complete gentleman. You have my word.''

She hesitated. Should she? On one hand she'd love to go. She could read it in his eyes, hear it in his voice and feel it in the air between them. He wanted her to go with him. He wanted her company. Not as a housekeeper, but as a woman.

As a woman he cared about?

"I'd love to." She shouldn't have said it that way, but when he smiled, she felt it all the way to the depth of her being.

Days later when Alexandra was waiting for Hailey's swimming lesson to finish, she tried not to let her imagination get away from her. It was too easy during the warm sunny days to believe John might feel for her the same way that she felt for him. Since he *did* invite her on the camping trip.

It was scary to feel this way about a man again. But John was different from any man she'd ever known. He was good to the core. Everyone said so. The friends she'd made in the Bible Study group told her one story after another of his brave rescues on the county's search and rescue team. He was the town's volunteer fire chief, always with a hand out to help.

No doubt about it. John was a good man. He had a good heart. He would make a fantastic husband.

What if John was ready to marry again? Sitting in the shade of a park bench, she closed her book thoughtfully. What if he *was* falling in love with her?

"Alexandra!" It was Michelle from the Bible Study group. "I thought that was you. Hey, I wanted to tell you that choir practice is today at seven. Kirby and I decided we'd better stop by to pick you up. It'll be harder to say no with both of us pressuring you, right?"

"Right."

"Hey, have you ever thought about a different haircut?" Michelle, one of the town beauticians, ran her fingers through the ends of Alexandra's hair.

"When you get a chance, come sneak down to the Snip & Style. I'll give you a courtesy cut."

"Some people might be wary of a free haircut."

"Oh, right. Well, I'll try not to shave you bald or scorch your scalp with the curling iron. I've never done that before, but there's always a first time, I guess."

"Sure. That makes me feel better."

"Thought it would. Sorry, I couldn't resist teasing. See you tonight!" Michelle trotted away.

The distant din of children's voices grew louder as the classes let out. The walkway became crowded as moms and their kids arrived for the next class. Alexandra tucked her paperback into her purse, soaking up the feel of this day. A toddler dashed past, running all-out, while a slim young woman shouted, "Travis, you come back here!" He ran harder, but his mother was faster. Laughing at her renegade son, she scooped the little boy up into her arms and he squealed.

She knew that not all families were like hers had been. It was reaffirming to see it.

"Alexandra!" Hailey skipped into sight, sandwiched between best friends Stephanie and Christa. "Can you take us for ice cream. Please? Please?"

"Yeah, please?" the girls echoed, all giving the best impressions of Bambi eyes Alexandra had ever seen.

"Ice cream is never a good idea. I highly disapprove." Alexandra winked, rising from the bench, and Hailey laughed, lunging against her waist, holding her hard in a sweet hug.

"I think you oughta get extra chocolate on your cone," Hailey told her. "'Cuz you're the bestest of them all."

"That's because I have a weakness for ice cream. Lucky for you." She pulled her keys from her shorts pocket. "C'mon, girls. It's my treat."

The three little girls shouted their approval, dashing through the crowd toward the faded yellow old Bug. They climbed in, debating who was going to sit in the back, then who was going to sit in the front, their cheer contagious.

"Hello, Alexandra," greeted a woman passing by, whom Alexandra recognized from the coffee shop.

"Hi, Helen." Surprised, she returned the older woman's smile as they went their separate ways.

It was unbelievable. Was she really starting to belong? It was a wonderful feeling.

"Hey, there, pretty lady."

She'd know that rich, chocolate-smooth voice anywhere. John. She turned around, trying so hard to hold on to her heart. How could she hold back her affection for him? An affection that grew every time she was with him. That doubled with every kind thing he did for her. "Hey, I thought you had a store to run."

"I left Warren in charge. He's working full-time for me now that school's out. I thought I'd sneak out and catch the last of Hailey's lesson." He shrugged one broad shoulder in apology. "I'm late."

"Hmm. Yes. Being late is a terrible offense. You'll have to pay for it."

"Let me guess. Judging by the way the girls are hanging out the window, wanting you to hurry, you're going to torture them with ice cream."

"Yep. I'm tough. You'd better not mess with me."

"I'll surrender without a fight."

"You just want chocolate. You can't fool me."

"It's not the chocolate I want."

Alexandra's heart skipped a beat as their gazes locked. Held. All around them the world kept turning. Kids dashing down the pathway, their towels fluttering out behind them. Mothers shouting to their children to mind the swim teacher and to meet right here when they were done.

The sound of engines starting, and vehicles chugging past and Hailey's anguished "Hurry up! We're dyin'!" was all part of the background, nothing but static that could not interrupt the single, perfect way John folded her hand in his.

The heat of his skin. The rough calluses that came with hard work. Sun browned, so dark against hers. So large against hers.

John was amazing. Everything he did made the world a better place, whether it was for his daughter or his mother and father or his community. He was good and kind and endlessly patient. Better than any man she'd ever known. And she wanted him with all the depth of her being.

She couldn't help it. She was falling hard and fast in love with him.

Chapter Eleven

As John was packing the tents into the back of his truck, he was still scolding himself. What he should have said to Alexandra was, "I wanted to check up with you and make sure you were all right."

"Dad, are you sure we can't take Angel?" Hailey skidded to a stop on the concrete and leaned against the side of his truck, so little girl in her bright purple T-shirt and her matching purple sunglasses. "We can still pick her up from Grammy's. Please? *Pleeease?*"

"She won't be safe," he told her for the four-teenth time in an hour. "Go get your backpack."

"But—" Hailey sighed dramatically, enough to make any Oscar winner proud, and stomped off to the house.

His patience was wearing thin today, no doubt about that. Alexandra should be here any minute—He looked over his shoulder. There she was, driving into sight. Now would be a great time to grab the tent from inside the garage—from way in the back and look really busy.

He retreated, figuring keeping busy would help him forget how Alexandra kept gazing up at him the other day outside the ice-cream shop. Exactly the same way she was looking at him now.

"Hi." She could dim the sun with the way she looked, dressed in a lemon-yellow tank top and denim shorts, her slender feet encased in chunky brown hiking boots that had seen better days. On her they looked perfect. She looked perfect.

He tore his gaze away. She may be perfect, but she wasn't right for him.

Remember that, John. He tugged the tent from its resting place between the rafters. A stake tumbled loose and hit him in the head. "Ow," he said as it crashed to the cement floor. "I nearly KO'd myself. That takes talent."

"John!" She dropped the duffel slung over her shoulder and jogged over to him, bringing the sunshine with her. "Oh, you're bleeding. Let me—"

She reached out, and he did his best to duck. But his ears were ringing a little and his balance was a little off. Pain pounded through the top of his skull, but he had a feeling it didn't have much to do with the blow to his head. It had everything to do with the woman running her fingertips across his scalp.

"I don't feel a lump. Yet. Let's get you sitting down, and I'll run for some ice."

Now he was really feeling foolish. If he'd had his mind on what he was doing and not on the beautiful lady in his garage, he wouldn't be bleeding right now.

Then again, she wouldn't be at his side. For once, he wanted to let Alexandra fuss over him. To kiss away the pain. To touch him with those fingers that stroked away all the anguish and tension, leaving only peace.

He didn't deserve peace. What he ought to be thinking about was how he was going to help this woman. That was his sworn duty to himself, to Alexandra and to the Lord. What had happened to his self-discipline that he couldn't control his own thoughts? Instead of wanting to protect her, he wanted to haul her against his chest and kiss her.

And she wouldn't stop touching him. Those tender fingers on his brow made him think about how tenderhearted she was. What a fine wife she would make.

See? This wasn't good, and it had to stop. He caught her slim wrist, meaning to stop her from touching him. But instead, he was touching her. Felt the fine bones of her wrist beneath his fingertips and the warm silk of her skin.

She was wholesome and trusting and good and had no idea what he was thinking. She whipped out a folded handkerchief from her pocket and moved in. Didn't she know what she was doing to him? The wall around his heart was crumbling danger- ously and her gentle ministrations could be enough to bring the whole thing tumbling down. He squeezed his eyes shut, fighting for control. He *would not* think about kissing her.

"There." She squinted, studying his brow. "The bleeding's stopped. I think you'll live."

Live? She was killin' him! She speared him deep. The defensive wall around his heart didn't stop her none. She made him feel. She made him want to love her.

Love her? Alexandra needed his protection. That's what he had to concentrate on. That's what was important here.

She smiled, and the cracks in the wall around his heart grew bigger. Just like that. You'd think a man like him, who wasn't afraid of scaling mountains with nothing more than a rope, would be so quick to crumble. It sure bothered him.

"Here, turn your head to the right. That's it." She was totally focused now as she peeled back the wrapping on a bandage she'd rescued from the first-aid box on the garage shelf.

He'd do just about anything, so long as she stayed with him. She pressed a bandage to his brow, just beneath the hairline, and her sweet scent enveloped him.

Her goodness shone when she took his hand. "I don't think that blow to the head was enough to give you a concussion."

"I'm a tough guy. I don't get concussions."

"I'm not fooled one bit, mister." Her fingers curled around his and squeezed. "You're not tough. You're tender. Wow."

Alexandra let go, her face flaming. Had she really said that? She couldn't believe it. She hightailed it out of the garage and headed straight for her car. She dug around for her sleeping bag and pillow and carried both to the back of the truck.

Was it too late to escape? She wasn't ready for this, and she wasn't sure she could believe in it. Was she going to get her heart broken, falling in love with a man like John?

"Let me help you with that." Suddenly he was at her elbow, as dependable as the mountains that rimmed the valley. He lifted the bundle from her arms with ease.

"Wait. You have a spot of blood—" She couldn't resist reaching out to touch him again.

The fine satin of his hair teased her knuckles, and the heat of his skin against her fingertips was amazing. She swiped at the speck of drying blood with the pad of her thumb. It felt intimate, to take care of him like this, and to be so close to him.

His eyes grew dark and his gaze traveled down her face and settled on her lips. Held.

He's going to kiss me. Alexandra couldn't think of anything else. Not the pillow she dropped or that they were visible from the house, where Hailey was. All she could think about was the way he inched ever closer, his gaze a touch that made her bottom lip tingle in anticipation. She wanted to share that sweetness with him.

Closer. His lips parted ever so slightly, and she did the same. She knew that his kiss would be tender and heartfelt. She also knew without asking that he hadn't kissed anyone since his wife.

And he cares about me. Encouraged, she closed her eyes at the first brush of his lips to hers. Gentle. Just as she'd known his kiss would be. Perfect.

The ricochet of the front door slamming broke them apart. Alexandra took a step back, lost in her own feelings as John turned abruptly and rearranged the camping gear in the truck bed.

The kiss had lasted only a few seconds, but it had been enough for her to know for sure. He did feel the same way about her. This wonderful, good-to-the-core man *did* care for her.

It was unbelievable.

"I'm glad you're here," he said.

"Me, too." Her heart felt full as Hailey burst into sight, dropped her backpack on the ground and wrapped her arms around Alexandra's waist. What a blessed feeling, to have this child's affection.

"I'm all packed and stuff. Guess what? Grammy took me shopping last night and I bought stuff for s'mores. I like 'em all mooshy, but not burned. Dad burns the marshmallows."

"He's a marshmallow burner? Shocking."

"I confess it. I'm a real man. If we eat marshmallows, then they'd better be charred and crisped." John winked as he scooped Hailey's pack into the back of the truck.

A real man. Yes, he was certainly that. Alexandra's spirits soared. This real man, good to the core, wanted to kiss her again. She felt certain of it.

And she was going to let him. It scared her, to think of trusting another man so deeply again. But looking at John as he told Hailey that they weren't going to stop and see Angel on the way out, Alexandra couldn't be too afraid. Even when he was annoyed, he kept his calm and his sense of humor. She loved him more for that, her very own white knight.

As if he could read her thoughts, he took her hand to help her into the truck. His touch made her heart soar.

Hailey chattered all the way, nearly nonstop, talking about everything while John drove with a bemused expression. They took the highway toward the mountains that were so close, Alexandra had to tip her head back to see their proud, jagged peaks.

"Sorry you came?" John asked in a split-second pause of Hailey's conversation.

"I'm so suffering." She didn't want to be anywhere else. This was paradise, sheer perfection, and she wanted to cherish every moment.

Then again, any moment spent with John was bliss. The kiss hung in the air between them, the knowledge of it and the tenderness. It could only mean one thing—that he wanted her in his life.

Joy filled her up slowly, the way dawn came to the mountains. Love moved that way, quiet and true. She felt changed because of it. Look what her future could be. John and Hailey could be her family. This could be her life.

"I love my new sleeping bag," Hailey announced. "It's all soft and has stuff inside—"

"Most people call it fleece," John clarified.

"And it's snugly, and my feet don't get cold if my socks get wet, 'cuz I fell in the river or somethin' like that one time…" She went on and on, each story more darling than the next until Alexandra ached with happiness.

This is what a family could be. This right here. It was no fantasy, no daydream, but it was as real as an answered prayer all around her. The sound of a happy child who'd never known neglect or abuse. The capable presence of a man who loved and lived in accordance to the Lord's word, which he held dear.

We could be happy together, she realized. Everything she'd ever wanted was right here. Within her reach.

Too full to speak, Alexandra didn't say a word. She let the harmony of being with John gladden her. Hailey chattered, John added comments and Alexandra wanted to hold on to each moment forever. She wanted them to add up to a lifetime.

"This is the end of the road. Now the fun begins." John guided the truck off the paved road. Low branches slapped against the truck's high fenders.

"You call this fun? Running into trees?"

"No, the fun is in avoiding the trees. Watch." They were going four-wheeling. One of John's favorite things.

The old logging road was overgrown, hardly visible between the break in the trees that ribboned up the hillside and out of sight. Just the way he liked it.

He put the truck in four-wheel drive. "Hold on."

Alexandra grabbed the door rail, laughing as the truck bumped and rocked over the rugged terrain. Not dangerous, but it was exhilarating. Hailey squealed, straining against her seat belt to watch as a young sapling hit the bumper and slid beneath the truck with a scraping sound.

"Look! A cougar!" Hailey pointed. "Oops. It ran away. There was this one time, when Dad and I hiked, and…"

He listened, delighted, as always, by his little girl and her exuberant spirit. But what he really noticed was Alexandra seated on the other side of the truck, her eyes shining with excitement.

Good. He wanted her to be happy. He sure liked her being here, with them. He tried not to think about the kiss they'd shared. It was brief, sweet. Friendly. Right?

Okay, he was trying to fool himself. There was nothing friendly about the kiss he'd given Alexandra. It had been tender. He'd kissed her with his whole heart. With a heart he had no right to offer her. *Lord, please help me to remember that.*

Resolved, he kept his attention on the faint tracks of the road hidden by thickets of grass and brush. Until the truck followed a curve into a clearing, and

Alexandra's gasp of amazement as the perfect peaks of the Bridger Mountains swept into sight. Strong, jagged, enduring.

He tried not to pick out the peak far to the left—he deliberately kept his gaze to the right, toward Alexandra. Maybe that was no coincidence. The fortress walls he'd built around his heart remained intact, but they were weakening. He had the terrible fear Alexandra could make them crumble.

Did he turn away from her? No. He could see only her. Her sparkle. Her gentle spirit. Her compassionate, loving nature as she climbed out of the truck, according to Hailey's instructions, and held out a hand to help the little girl to the ground.

"Dad and I hike a whole lot," Hailey was saying as she slipped her sunglasses off of her nose. "Did you hike with your dad?"

"Nope. My dad wasn't around much."

"Christa's dad is divorced and lives in Missoula. He ain't around much, either."

So trusting, Hailey's fingers crept into Alexandra's hand. John's throat constricted watching the two of them. They could be mother and daughter, with the way they were both slim, both graceful, both sparkling like sunlight on a mountain stream.

"I'm so happy." Hailey tipped her head back, causing her golden blond locks to tumble away from her face. "Very, very happy. Come with me, Alexandra. I know the way."

"What about your dad? I guess we can forget him. He's just the chauffeur."

"We'd better bring him," Hailey gleefully teased. "He's good at packing stuff and he can put up the tent."

"A useful man. All right, then, we'll allow him to come. But only if he can keep up with us wild girls."

"Yeah!" Hailey giggled. "Hurry up, Dad."

"I'm coming. Golly." He locked the cab and swung around to the back. "You wild girls look like you have a lot of energy. Here. You'd better carry the heavy pack."

"But I'm the littlest." Hailey shoved her glasses onto her nose, a precious sprite that smiled up at him with Bobbie's grin. "He's just teasing, Alexandra."

"Me? Tease? I'm dead serious." He hefted the big pack, with the heavy gear, out of the back of the truck bed and offered it to her. "Here, Alexandra. Since I'm just the chauffeur, not the pack mule."

"Oh, you have other uses, too."

It would be so easy to draw her into his arms and hold her sheltered and safe against his chest. Simple to give in to the tenderness he longed to feel for her.

Maybe he could give in. Just a little.

"I'm so glad you invited me." She eased into her backpack. "I can't wait to get started. How far are we going to hike in?"

"About two miles. Can you make it?"

"Me? Sure. The question is, can you?"

"Questioning my strength and endurance, are you? I'm not the most decorated member of the county's search and rescue team for nothing."

"Sure, go ahead and brag. You've never been up against me before."

"Is that a challenge? I have to warn you. I'm a competitive kind of guy. I play to win."

"Ooh, me, too. Last one there has to put up the tents." She quirked one brow, eyeing him up and down as if she wasn't impressed with what she saw. "Prepare to eat our dust."

"It's grassy. There is no dust." He slid his arms into the padded straps, letting the heavy weight of the pack settle along his back. "Go ahead. I'll give you a head start. You're going to need it."

"Awfully confident, aren't you?"

"Sure. I'm an awfully confident guy. I always get what I want."

"Then what are you waiting for?" She held out her hand.

His fingers slipped through hers as if they were made to be there. Hand in hand. Her smaller palm fit inside his perfectly. He felt another rend in the wall protecting his heart. He knew it was wrong, but he held on to her, matching his longer stride to hers as they headed shoulder to shoulder into the forest.

"Hurry, Alexandra! Dad's gonna beat us!"

"I'm hurrying." She was out of wind.

Okay, so John was in excellent shape. One look at his amazing physique would tell her that, but she *had* to win. The climb was uphill, and the rocks kept crumbling beneath her boots. It didn't help that John grabbed hold of her backpack and playfully held her in place.

"No fair." She twisted away, but he took advantage, sprinting past her on the narrow ridge. "You get a penalty for that unnecessary roughness, buddy."

"What kind of penalty?"

"I don't know. You're already in trouble with me."

"Me? In trouble? Impossible. I'm a good guy. Innocent. I don't cause trouble."

"I don't have your mom's potato salad recipe, do I? Nope. Someone broke his word to me on that."

"I couldn't get it. Mom's ruthless when it comes to her secret recipe."

"Fine, but you *are* her son. You have an inside track."

"You might think so, but my mom said she'd give it to me if I married, and not until."

"Well, if that's what it takes." She caught hold of his backpack and tugged enough to slow him down.

He fell in line beside her. "Hey! You're stronger than you look."

"You just remember that when you're putting up the tents, loser." She shouldered past, gaining the lead. "You'll be working to the sweat while Hailey and I soak our feet in the creek. Right, Hailey?"

"Yep. Unless there's bugs 'n stuff." Hailey led the way, being the experienced hiker she was. "Ooh, that's where we always camp."

"C'mon, Hailey, let's run." She grabbed the little girl's hand, and they laughed together, trying to get ahead as John swept his daughter off her feet.

"Hey, Dad!"

"Maybe we'll be soaking our toes while Alexandra does the tents." John swung his daughter to his chest and held her tight, awkward backpack and all, and her merry giggle lifted on the breeze, echoing across the rugged peaks of the mountains all around them. "C'mon, kid. We're gonna win."

"Oh, yeah?" Alexandra dug down deep. It was hard to admit she was tired from the several miles' walk at high altitude, but she wasn't about to let John beat her. She had her reputation to uphold! She started running. He glanced over his shoulder, saw she was gaining and ran harder.

"Oh, no!" She wasn't going to lose. She sprinted all-out, chugging past him, her backpack clunking against her lower back as she shot ahead and into a mountain meadow lush and green.

An elk lifted its head, heavy rack of antlers pointing into the sky, and took off in a streak of brown into the trees.

"Already scaring off the neighbors." Out of breath, John eased Hailey to the ground. "That poor elk is running back to his family to tell them the neighborhood is going downhill, now that the humans have moved in."

"Or he's telling the hungry bears where to find us."

"Not used to being so remote?"

There was no sign of civilization anywhere. The velvety texture of trees on the high slope, the soar of an eagle overhead and the echoing presence of nature that felt vast and powerful. She felt small against such greatness, and enlivened, too. "I've never been anywhere like this, and I'm a country girl."

"Then you like it?"

"Love it." She breathed deep, taking in the crisp mountain air and gazing at God's beautiful handi-

work. "I could get used to having elk for my neighbors."

"That's why we come up here all the time." John
took her hand in his, big, warm, strong.

She felt the connection between them deep in her
heart.

"You go dip your toes in the creek and rest up."
John squeezed her fingers gently, tenderly, before he
moved away. "Since Hailey and I are big losers,
we'll put up the tents."

"I didn't lose," Hailey protested gaily. "You
grabbed me up and I couldn't help it."

"Sometimes life isn't fair." John ruffled his
daughter's hair, all affection, and all unshakable fatherly protection. "C'mon. Let's show Alexandra
how it's done. She might be a country girl, but she
doesn't know how it's done in Montana."

When John brushed a kiss on Alexandra's cheek,
hope rose within her, growing with every beat of
her heart.

"Is she asleep?" Alexandra whispered over the
crackle of the fire as John emerged from the dark.

"As soon as her head hit the pillow." He swung
his leg over the log and hunkered down next to her.
"She ate so many s'mores, it's a shock she could
actually sleep."

"Me, too. I'm in the throes of a sugar high."

Alexandra reached into the open plastic bag and fished out another marshmallow. "You might as well join me."

"How can I resist the temptation?" He held out his hand, palm up, for the fluffy treat. "Having fun yet?"

"You could call it that." She'd had the best day. Exploring the mountainside with Hailey, searching for the wild roses that bloomed in early summer. Letting John hold her hand as they walked in the meadow, watching an eagle soar overhead and the elk return to see if his grazing spot was still full of humans.

"I'm glad." John pierced the marshmallow with the end of a willow stick he'd carved earlier, one for each of them. "Not too many women like to hang out in the backcountry."

"I'm one of those rare women, I guess," she said lightly, teasing.

"I'll say." He wasn't teasing. "You haven't complained once."

"What's to complain about?"

"No running water, no warm water and no indoor plumbing, for a start."

"I love those things, believe me. But isn't this something?" She gazed up at the sky above, the stars so thick and close she felt as if she could gather them up in her hands.

"This is something." John wasn't looking at the heavens.

He was gazing at her. In the flickering firelight, he was completely exposed. His guard down. She could see past his tender heart into the goodness of his soul.

She could sense his thoughts even before he leaned closer. Before his gaze focused on her waiting lips. His eyes grew as dark as dreams as he waited, the air buzzing between them, the infinite night and the diamond sky witnesses as he dipped to cover her mouth with his.

His kiss was like moonlight, silvered and rare. Like the gentlest brush of nightfall. It was like coming home and finding forever all in one sweet touch. His kiss was pure tenderness and all heart.

His kiss made her ache all the way to the bottom of her heart with a love so fierce and pure, she couldn't stop it. Couldn't deny it. Couldn't make these powerful, wonderful feelings stop. Not even when he broke the kiss, staying close to gaze into her eyes, and their souls touched.

Chapter Twelve

Alexandra snuggled into her sleeping bag, trying as hard as she could not to make any sound and wake Hailey. The little girl slumbered in her own sleeping bag, turned on her side so that all Alexandra could see of her was the fall of blond hair across her pillow.

It was cozy being here like this. Sweet. Humbling. With John's kiss still tingling on her lips, with the connection between them still unbroken, she dared to think about a future with John. With the man she loved.

This really is love, she realized. A love like she'd never known before. A power of love she never knew existed.

It was like the passage from Corinthians. John's

love was patient and kind. It did not demand its own way. He was not jealous or proud, boastful or rude.

This was her new day, her new opportunity with John. This was her one chance at a happily-ever-after. At a hope and the future the Lord promised. Was John planning to propose?

Thank you for leading me here, Father. She was grateful with all she was and all she had. If this love she and John shared could blossom and grow into a marriage and a life together, then she would never ask for anything else. What would she need? She would already have everything that mattered. Hailey would be her daughter. Her very own daughter. John would be the love of her life. A true soul mate. And later there would be babies. Precious gifts from the Father above to celebrate their beautiful love.

Sure, she was getting ahead of herself, but she could see the future like a bright glittering star right there on the horizon, ready to rise into the sky and shine brighter than any other star in the heavens. That's how wonderful her future was going to be as John's wife.

Happy tears burned in her eyes and wet her face. Every trial she'd been through in her life was worth it, because it made her who she was. Her hardships had brought her here, to John's loving arms. She had everything she'd ever prayed for. Ever wanted. Would ever dream of.

Love filled her, true and pure, generous and kind, unconditional and infinite. She lay long into the night, dreaming—just dreaming of how her future with John would be—until sleep carried her away.

I shouldn't have done that, Lord. I never should have kissed Alexandra for real. Full on the lips. And meant it. John buried his face in his hands. What had he been thinking? He wasn't thinking—that was the problem. He'd been acting on his feelings. On the bright, singular affection that was too beautiful for the likes of him to be feeling.

I know I don't deserve another chance at paradise, Lord. But if I had the right to take Alexandra as my wife, I'd protect her always. Cherish her more than any man could love his wife. If I could only deserve such a gift as her love.

John couldn't bring himself to ask for such a blessing from the Lord. He didn't have to close his eyes to see the image; it was already flashing through his mind. The rope breaking with a snap. The whip of the broken rope against the sheet of granite and Bobbie's cry as she started to fall. He'd been rehammering a piton because the rock was stubborn and Bobbie hadn't gotten it in deep enough. In the second it took for him to figure out what was going on and grab the safety, she'd already plunged past him. Bobbie! The rope jerked tight with her weight. Saving her.

Adrenaline had electrified him, and he started dragging her up, hand over hand, thankful the piton held her safe. She dangled ten feet below him, gazing up with fear stark on her face, the plea in her eyes unmistakable. The valley floor stretched out over three thousand feet below.

"Hold on to the rock." But it was too late. The piton broke away, he was off balance and he couldn't keep ahold of her hand. Her glove started to peel away...

Lord, I can't remember this. I can't relive that moment again. John squeezed his eyes shut, praying for the images to vanish. He breathed hard, fighting until the memory cleared.

He'd died that day, too. Every prayer he made, every Sunday service he attended, every time he opened a Bible, there it was. The one thing he could not be forgiven for. The shame and horror that he could not face. Could not bear to look at. And what was worse, was that God knew. God, who knew every failure, right there, hiding in John's soul.

There was no way he could deserve Alexandra or her precious love.

John sat on the log and stared at the embers that

had been their campfire. Watched as the glow faded from the embers until there was only ashes and darkness.

Alexandra woke to the symphony of birdsong that proceeded the dawn, as if a thousand birds of every kind were singing to the eastern horizon, calling the sun to rise. Who could sleep through that much noise? Apparently Hailey could. Alexandra punched her pillow and closed her eyes. It was no good. Slumber eluded her because she was thinking about John.

What a kiss. What a man. Remembering, Alexandra felt joy fill her in a slow, warm sweep. A wonderful glow filled her, a contented happiness unlike anything she'd ever known. She couldn't wait to see him. Could he be up this early?

It wasn't sunrise, but she was going to find out. Besides, if she'd lie here tossing and turning, she might wake Hailey. No sense in doing that, so she slipped out of her sleeping bag and unzipped the tent flap.

John's pup tent looked silent as she refastened the flap and pulled her sweatshirt on over her shirt. He *could* be asleep in there. She felt alone. The wind had a bite to it, and she shivered. Maybe she could get a fire going and start a pot of coffee—

Something moved in the shadows. A man's wide shoulders and straight back. It was John. He sat with his elbows on his knees, hands together, watching the eastern horizon. With his back to her, he didn't know she was there.

What a man. She couldn't help admiring him, this good man she'd fallen in love with. He heard the pad of her step and his spine straightened.

"Good morning, handsome." She wrapped her arms around his neck from behind.

He stiffened and for an entire minute, he didn't move. Then his hands braced her forearms and he unwound her from his throat. "Good morning."

He sounded pretty gruff. Alexandra felt slapped. Didn't John want her affection? That hadn't been the story last night. Maybe he didn't sleep well.

Or perhaps he regretted their kiss.

No, that couldn't be true. John had held her with incredible tenderness. It had been no accident, but a deliberate act of love. It couldn't be faked.

But it could be regretted.

Alexandra stumbled. She felt as if the earth had disappeared beneath her feet. Last night she'd thought he would want a life with her. But now...

No, maybe he's tired or not feeling well. She'd *felt* the love in his heart. She *knew* it was there.

What she needed to do was to figure out what was troubling him. She would make it right, whatever it was. She settled down beside him. "Did you get much sleep?"

"Nope."

His gaze was shuttered. So was his heart. Different from last night. He was like he'd been when they first met. Distant. Brooding. Unreachable. What was wrong? "Did the owl keep you up?"

"I'm used to owls."

"The deer were pretty loud grazing in the meadow. I woke up to the sound of them chewing right outside the tent."

"I'm used to deer, too."

Not a good sign. "Was it our kiss? You regret it. Oh, you do." She watched in horror as he turned away, as if ashamed and weighted down by regret.

"It never should have happened. I wasn't thinking. I had no right to kiss you. None at all. I know what you think. You're hoping there's a future in this. But I have to be honest. I can't lie to you, Alexandra. I never meant—" He turned away, tendons cording in his throat, muscles straining in his jaw. "It won't happen again."

"I see." Her heart began to splinter into a billion tiny shards, so sharp-edged, the pain left her breathless and reeling. John didn't want her. He didn't want her kiss.

Those dreams of a future as John's wife lifted like soap bubbles into the air and popped into nothing at all. She hid her face in her hands, embarrassed and ashamed. Way to go, Alexandra. He had to know she was in love with him. She'd shown him her heart. Why didn't he love her?

Her mother's words reeled into her mind like a whisper from the mountaintops. *Don't think you'll grow up to be no different than me, Alexandra… Who's gonna love you?*

Oh, John. I thought you could. I thought— She launched off the log and fisted her hands, walking hard. Embarrassment burned hot as flame in her soul as she took refuge in the shadows.

Pain slashed through her, sharper than any blade could ever cut. Her hand flew to her chest, but it couldn't stop the agony ripping through her. Nothing in her life had ever hurt like this. Not one thing. Worse, it was all her fault. She'd wanted John so much. She loved him, heart and soul.

She'd needed a hero. A white knight to save her from her past. From the hurt Patrick had put into her heart and from the lost little girl she'd been, craving a bright, sheltering love.

She'd been a fool. At least, that's how she felt. Shame burned her face, and she was grateful for the dark. Glad John couldn't see her.

"Alexandra." His voice came from directly behind her.

Oh, Lord, don't let him see me like this. Don't let him guess how wrong I've been. He can't know how deeply I love him. She desperately needed some scrap of pride to hold on to.

Then he touched her, curling his hand around her shoulder. Making the agony inside her bleed.

"I'm sorry. If it helps, I'd like to marry you. If I could."

"No, that doesn't help." It was worse.

He pulled her into his arms. His embrace was the shelter she'd always craved. His love the soft place she'd always yearned for. She leaned into him, letting him take some of her pain, allowing him to be her comfort.

He smelled like woodsmoke and pine needles, and the soft fleece of his sweatshirt caressed the side of her face. With her ear against his chest, she listened to him breathe and to the rapid beat of his heart. Thumping fast and hard and hollow. She never wanted to let him go.

"You are a wonderful woman." His hand curled around her nape, his fingers tender on her vulnerable spine as he cradled her against him. "You deserve a man with a whole heart to give you."

"I'd take whatever you could spare."

"No." He brushed his lips against her temple, a tender and brief kiss that would be their last. "You don't understand. You don't know what I am."

"You are my protector and my friend. You are the most noble man I've ever met."

John felt as if an ax was cleaving his heart in two. He hated seeing the depth of her love for him, glittering in her like a rare and precious gem. Her heart was so open and so easy to read. How could he turn away? He wanted her love more than anything on this planet. He wanted her with his entire soul. "I'm not so noble."

"Yes, you are. After all this time, you're still in love with your wife."

It would be easy to let her think that. Then he'd never risk losing her love. She'd never know the kind of man he was. Never look at him and see less than the protector she thought him to be.

He loved Alexandra. With his entire being. With all he was and all he had. If he could simply hold her in his arms, keep her nestled against his heart and feel her gentle love wrap around him, then he knew this agony in his soul would end. She could make his guilt disappear. She could be the balm to soothe the mortal wounds in his past.

He didn't need to tell her the truth. All he had to do was to tell her that he loved her. He could still fix this. He wanted to be weak, not noble, to hold on to her forever so this soul-rending pain would end.

But it wasn't right. It wasn't fair. Alexandra deserved a better man than he could be. Ever.

Forcing her away from him felt as if he were ripping his heart out of his chest without the benefit of anesthesia, but it had to be done. He took a deep breath and gathered what remained of his integrity.

"I'm not still in love with my wife," he confessed. "I'm responsible for her death."

"No." Alexandra's denial was fierce and instantaneous.

"I wasn't strong enough to hold her. To keep her from falling."

"John, that's not true. You aren't in control of life and death. Only God is."

"You weren't there." She stubbornly wanted to believe the best in him, and he wasn't going to let her. "I couldn't find it in me to keep my wife from falling three thousand feet to her death. I should have been able to save her, and I couldn't. My heart fell right along with her, all three thousand feet, and crashed to the ground. I can't love you. I can't."

He marched off, leaving her in the shadows, as the sun rose, a peachy gold smudge over the mountains. Watching John walk away was the toughest thing she'd ever done. God gave her strength as she swiped at the wetness on her cheeks, willing no more tears to fall.

She was strong enough for this. God had led her here to show her that. She took a deep breath, and felt wounded and whole all at once. Loving John had given her a strength she didn't know she had. Strength she would need in order to let him go.

It was over between them. There had never been a chance for them. Ever.

Raw emotion left her trembling as she eased to her knees in the tall grass. Hidden by the shadows, she covered her face with her hands and let the hot, burning tears come. The pain in her heart did not end, even after the tears had run dry.

She knew it never would.

Patrick Kline eased up on the accelerator, not bothering to signal as he cut across two lanes of traffic and zipped onto the off-ramp just in time. Might as well check this last exit. Being the ambitious attorney came in handy most of the time—he'd learned to be thorough and logical. He'd checked the gas stations, convenience stores and campgrounds off every exit since Seattle.

He'd find her. There wasn't a woman who could outsmart him, and Alexandra didn't come close to having his intelligence. One of God's blessings that Patrick used with great pride.

A sign caught his eye. The Lazy J Campground. Vacancy. Looked like a dirt-cheap place. Alexandra was on a tight budget. He'd check there first.

Chapter Thirteen

It had been another sleepless night. John filled his travel coffee cup, almost brimming it over because he was so tired. The night on the mountain had taken its toll. He felt raw and wounded and bleeding. He feared not even prayer could make this pain fade.

Ten to eight. It looked as if he'd better get a move on. Alexandra would be here any minute. She always came a few minutes early. With any luck, he'd be in his truck, ready to leave when she drove into sight.

"Dad!" Hailey was already outside on her horse. "Can I go to Stephanie's later?"

"Take that up with Alexandra." Even saying her name was painful.

You're falling apart, John. Don't think about her

and you'll be all right. That was a lie. He was never going to be all right again. No woman had ever burrowed so deep inside his heart. This love he felt for Alexandra was greater than the distance from the earth to the moon. He feared it could reach all the way to heaven.

You can't have her, John. He knew it—and the truth tore him apart. The image of Bobbie's face that last moment he'd been able to hold on to her didn't leave him as he stumbled out the door.

"Know what, Dad?" Hailey guided her horse to the driveway, where she sat bareback in a pair of jeans and a fringed shirt. "I had the best time and stuff, you know, with Alexandra. And if, like, you wanted to get married like Grammy says you should, then you can just marry Alexandra. She's like a real mom!"

Could the blade stuck in his heart dig any deeper? Anguished, John yanked open the door, spilling coffee all over his boots and the gravel driveway. Great, and here came Alexandra. Pulling up in her little car, windows down to enjoy the temperate morning, her hair tousled around her face, making her look wholesome and beautiful and exactly like the kind of woman he could never deserve.

It took all his steely willpower to turn his back and climb into the truck. He lifted a hand in a casual wave to Alexandra, as if she were merely the housekeeper and not the love of his life and the missing piece to his soul.

He couldn't look at her as he drove away.

Their friendship was ruined, too. Sorrow felt like lead as she watched John's truck disappear around the bend. As if he couldn't get away from her fast enough. She parked her car in the shade, waved to Hailey as the girl rode her horse over and tried not to let the sinking feeling in her chest take her mood any lower.

Is it going to be like this from now on?

John's love and a future with him had been devastating to lose. But his friendship, too? How could she go without that? How could she go back to baby-sitting Hailey when she'd hoped Hailey would become her stepdaughter?

What was she going to do?

Just concentrate on your work for today, Alexandra. Trust in the Lord to show you the way. So, after taking a deep breath and gathering her courage, she climbed out of the car. Instead of feeling at peace, she felt on edge. That was a loss, too. She treasured the sanctuary she'd once found here.

"Can I go to Stephanie's?" Atop her horse, Hailey remained at Alexandra's side on the trek across the driveway. "You don't have to drive me or nuthin'. I'm gonna ride over. We're gonna ride the trail down to the river and stuff. Can I, can I, please?''

''Sure. Let me give Stephanie's mom a call first.'' Alexandra tugged affectionately on the toe of Hailey's riding boot and was rewarded with a beaming smile.

Hailey dismounted, leading Bandit by the ends of the reins.

Something cold snaked down Alexandra's spine. Then it was gone. The morning was pleasant, the ever-present breeze warm. Uneasy, she glanced around her. She'd never noticed how much the giant lilacs and hedges could provide cover for someone lurking about.

Not that there was anyone lurking. It was just a weird way to feel suddenly. Probably more than anything else, it had to do with how raw her emotions were right now. Everything felt off-kilter. Although there was no chance at a marriage with John, he was still watching over her. Keeping her safe. The town sheriff had promised to do no less.

I'm pulled in too many directions, she thought while she waited for Hailey to tether her horse. It's being here in a small town. It's finding out I don't belong after all, just like when I was a little girl. It's this small town. She'd been a fool to stay. Small towns had never brought her anything but pain.

"I gotta get my stuff!" Hailey darted ahead, skipping through the house.

Alexandra's neck tingled again. She didn't feel right about that. She waited in the threshold, watching the world around her. Bandit stole bites of grass from the edge of the lawn, unconcerned. Nothing seemed out of place.

She shut the door and turned the dead bolt. They were probably safe as could be, but it never hurt to err on the side of safety. If Patrick hadn't found her by now, then he'd probably given up, right?

"Corey!" Cameron boomed into the store over the sound of the front door banging open. "You in here?"

"More or less." John straightened from the shelf he was restocking. "What can I do you for?"

"I'm not here as a customer." Cam's face was grim lines and a long, worried frown. "I spotted a car I didn't recognize. In-state plates, but something troubled me so I ran 'em. Stolen plates that didn't match the car. Figure you'd better put in a call to that nice Miss Sims out at your place. Just in case."

"I'll do it now." John's pulse kicked hard as he sprinted down the aisle and snagged the receiver from the wall unit. He punched in his home number, praying for Alexandra to be just fine, for this to have nothing to do with her.

The phone rang on and on. With no answer.

Maybe she was outside with Hailey. That didn't explain the bad feeling in his guts. Something was wrong. "I couldn't reach her."

"Could be a fair explanation for that." Cameron headed for the door. "She could be outside, or the line could be cut. You comin'?"

In a heartbeat. Without bothering to lock up, John walked out of the store. *Please, let her be safe, Lord. Let this be a scare.*

He couldn't lose Alexandra, too.

He hopped into the passenger seat of the patrol cruiser as Cam put the idling car in gear and tore out onto the street. He hit the lights, not the sirens, sending folks out of their way in a hurry.

Good. They had to get there fast. He had a bad feeling. Something wasn't right. Alexandra would have been in the house this time of morning....

I can't lose another woman I love. John sucked in a ragged breath. The agony in his heart doubled at the thought of anyone hurting Alexandra. The woman so precious to his heart. The one woman he wanted above all else. Above anyone. Ever.

Faster, he prayed as Cam hit the open highway at full speed.

Alexandra was rescuing the flour canister from the pantry shelf when she heard the muffled squeak.

Like a floorboard creaking beneath someone's weight. The hair at the back of her neck stood on end. An icy chill whipped through her as she turned from the pantry door, the puppy already barking.

Patrick. Alexandra froze, horror rooting her feet to the floor. Her muscles had turned to stone. She couldn't move. She couldn't think. All she saw was the gun in Patrick's raised hand. The cold gleam of black metal was aimed directly at her.

"No!" The single word was torn from her throat as fear turned to rage. She was across the kitchen floor in two seconds flat, protecting Hailey with her body. "Patrick, stay back. You're not welcome here."

"You don't know what I can do." There was darkness in Patrick's words—fury, anger and the will to do harm. "Do you want to see?"

"No! Don't hurt us." She had to think, and think fast. First priority was to get Hailey away from Patrick. "Please, just lower the gun. You don't need it. I'll do anything you want. Let's just leave, okay?"

"Glad you've finally decided to see things my way." His dark hatred felt as deadly as the gun he shook at her. "Then you're sorry?"

"Y-yes." She fought panic. She wouldn't be afraid of him. He'd taken enough from her, and she'd won it back. She refused to give it up again. "I'm ready. Let's go now."

There had once been kindness in Patrick, but now there was only lethal fury as his thumb dug into the tender flesh beneath her collarbone and his fingertips pierced in her neck. "Move."

Alexandra gritted her teeth against the piercing pain and willed her feet forward. Patrick pushed, nearly lifting her off the ground. She didn't cry out as the pain intensified, because she was too angry. Rage pumped through her as she stumbled toward the front door.

"Alexandra!" Hailey sounded terrified. But at least she'd be left behind. She'd be safe. That was all that mattered.

"Call your grammy," Alexandra choked out before Patrick's thumb squeezed the air out of her throat, cutting her off temporarily.

When he moved his thumb, they were outside and she gasped for breath. She twisted around, desperate to see inside the house. Hailey was so terrified. Was she all right?

Patrick flung her against his car door. "Forget the brat and get in."

"Fine. I told you. I'll be agreeable. Let's just leave." That would be best for Hailey. "Now, Patrick. Let's hurry."

"That's what frustrates me. You don't know your place. Believe me, you're finally going to learn," he said as he followed her into the car. He turned the ignition with his left hand, keeping a solid hold on the gun. Sunlight gleamed on its dark barrel. Patrick gunned the engine, and they flew along the driveway.

What was going to happen to her now? Patrick had slipped past the sheriff's defenses, and John was in town. She was alone. She had no weapon. She had nothing to fight with.

Wait—that wasn't true. She had faith. That's all she needed. God had brought her here, and He'd see her through. Somehow. Some way.

Suddenly Patrick swore. She saw flashing red and blue lights and the white bullet of a police cruiser taking the narrow lane way too fast. There was no room to pass. There were ditches and fencing on either side.

"Patrick!" She squeezed her eyes shut, bracing for the impact.

The car spun to the right, tires spinning dust and gravel. They were on Bev's driveway now, which intersected through the farm. The BMW flew low over the fields.

"Watch out!" Gerald's tractor lurched out of a field and onto the road. It was too late for either of them to stop.

Alexandra held on while the car soared into the potato fields, crushing new green clumps of the vegetable planted in tidy, endless rows as it landed. The seat belt cut into her neck but held her in place. Recovering control, Patrick pointed the hood straight down the field, dodging the rain of irrigation stands as he went.

Alexandra searched for the police car in the side-view mirror. She only saw dust pluming up like a tornado behind them. There he was!

John. He'd come for her. She rejoiced. He'd kept his word. He was her hero, her shining white knight who'd never break his promise to her. A man she could always depend on.

Sunlight glinted on Patrick's gun. The joy diminished. She changed her mind. She didn't want John here. He could be hurt or killed. *Protect him, Lord,* she prayed, watching the police cruiser fall behind and then out of sight in the side-view mirror.

John heard the gunshot ricochet through the river canyon as he leaped from the still-moving patrol car. His feet hit the ground with an impact hard enough to rattle the marrow from his bones, but he was already running past the abandoned BMW. Already fearing the worst. *I'm too late. I can't save her. It's too late.*

He dimly heard Cam shout his name, but he was beyond anything but getting to where that gunshot came from. He raced past the abandoned car. Alexandra's slip-on sneaker was on the ground. Blood marked the white canvas side. Alexandra's blood.

The sight of it ripped at his soul. If there was any hope, if she was wounded, then as God was his witness he was going to save her from the next bullet. He wasn't going to fail her. He *couldn't* fail her.

He tore along the narrow path, where drops of blood stained the wild grasses. His hopes exploded like a lit keg of dynamite when he saw her on the steep cliffside ahead of him, climbing for cover as the man following her steadied a handgun, aimed and squeezed the trigger.

"Alexandra!"

John's warning reverberated along the river canyon below her. Alexandra's foot slipped, rocks tumbled beneath the sole of her one shoe and she fell, hitting her knees on sharp rock. A bullet stirred the air a few inches from her left ear. More rocks slid out from under her. She dug her fingertips into the earth and rock to keep from sliding.

It was a long way down. All she could see was the sloping crest of the canyon wall falling several hundred feet down to the silver thread of the river below. Exposed and open, there was no place to hide. Patrick had a clear shot.

She'd enraged him when she'd knocked the gun aside when he'd stopped the car. The gun had tumbled to the floorboards and with one quick leap into the field, she was out of his reach, running even as a bullet had grazed her, slicing across her ankle. But it didn't stop her from escaping.

He was angrier now. Determined. She ducked, dropped and rolled. Letting gravity take her. Rocks and dirt scraped her bare thigh.

Faster. Gravity was pulling at her now, and she groped for a small tree, but the sapling snapped out of her fingers. She kept going, her bare foot striking a rock. Pain glanced up her shin, but it wasn't her main problem. The cliff side was becoming steeper.

She dug in, the earth tearing at her fingers. She couldn't stop. *Oh, Lord, please help me.* She was falling too fast, the grade growing steeper until all she could see was the riverbed below her bare feet. She could taste panic on her tongue, feel it in her wild heartbeat.

I really don't want to die today, Lord.

"Alexandra!" John's voice boomed, full of panic and terror. It reverberated along the canyon walls.

Lord, please hold her in the palm of Your hand. John was already running. No man with a gun was going to stop him. Cam shouted, trying to stop him, but it was too late. All John could see as he skidded down the steep grade was Alexandra tumbling behind an outcropping of rocks and out of sight.

No! She was gone. She was dead. Rage hammered through him as he took the slope at a run, letting his boots ski over earth and rock. The descent was fast—he braced his heels to absorb the shock as he skidded from the open face to a more protected outcropping of rocks. Above the pounding of blood in his ears, he heard the pop of a gun. A cold numb feeling blossomed in his left biceps. Crimson spread in a fast-moving circle on his sleeve.

He didn't care how badly he was shot. He had to get to Alexandra. His life wasn't worth anything if she wasn't alive. She was everything. And if she was gone... Grief lashed him hard as he reached the edge of the cliff, digging in with his heels, throwing his whole body back to stop his descent.

I should have loved her when I had the chance. Reached out and held her to me instead of shoving her away. If only I could have told her how much I love her. Heart and soul. For now and for eternity.

He crept over the cliff on his belly, already knowing what he was going to see. An empty canyon oddly silent with the feel of death.

"John." His name was a ragged whisper. He looked down into a pale, bloody woman's face a couple of feet below him. Her scraped hands were clutched tight around a spindly pine tree limb...one that looked ready to go at any minute.

Alexandra. He felt as high as heaven in one second. He read her fear. He saw the earth begin to move as the tree gave way.

He couldn't reach her. He crept out as far as he could go, stretched and touched air. Inches separated them. "Take my hand."

"I can't." She was on the edge of losing control. Panic flashed in her eyes. She looked up at him. Help me, she seemed to say. Save me.

Rocks tumbled. The tree gave, the roots breaking off, Alexandra began slipping.

"No!" Horror rose in the depths of his heart, from the breadth of his soul. A terrible image flashed back to him. One moment he was seeing Bobbie falling all over again, her hand outstretched to him, her fingers reaching for his as the distance between them grew. The pleading look in her eyes, the fear of death and pain stark on her pixie face.

As he had then, John dug down deep, asking for strength, gathering every bit of might he possessed, praying that Cam had caught up to Patrick. Tree and rock gave way and he snared Alexandra's wrist as the tree tumbled in a free fall along the jagged cliff wall.

His injured arm trembled with the strain, but he hauled her up and into his arms. Holding her tight and safe, never to let her go.

Thank you, Lord. John buried his face in Alexandra's neck, breathing in the scent of earth and apple shampoo. Tears burned in his eyes and ached in his throat. "I'm so thankful. Oh, baby, I thought I'd lost you."

"Me, too." She held him tight, sobbing now, clutching his shirt with both fists. "You saved me, John. You're so amazing. I love you so much. I just love you so much."

"Oh, my love." He kissed her hair, her cheeks, her lips. Life and death were in God's hands today, just as it had been those many years ago. It had been God's will, which only He could understand.

And it was God's will that Alexandra was safe in his arms, smiling up at him. She'd never looked so beautiful. So renewed. So serene. "I owe my life to you."

"Yep. You're in deep debt to me now." He kissed her forehead, then her lips. A soft, tender caress. "I'm going to have to think of a way to charge you for saving your life."

"How about free housecleaning for a month?"

"Hmm, I was thinking you might like to clean our house for the rest of your life."

"*Our* house? But you said—"

"Marry me, Alexandra." He kissed her again, feather-soft on her silky skin, and the tenderness inside him doubled. Fierce love burned in his chest for her, in his heart, in his soul. "I have never loved anyone the way I love you."

"I know just how you feel." Tears sparkled in

her eyes. Happiness lit her up as she kissed him gently. "How do you feel about a quick wedding?"

"The quicker the better. I can't wait to lift your veil. I want you for my wife."

Love lit him up inside, chasing away every last shadow, and the wall protecting his heart came crumbling down, every last piece as she buried her face in the hollow of his neck, holding tight, so very tight. She was heaven in his arms, so precious and amazing, and he intended to treasure her all the days of his life from this moment on.

Epilogue

"It was a beautiful ceremony." Bev appeared through the crowd, a glass of her special-recipe punch cradled in one hand. As the mother of the groom, she'd chosen a deep rose chiffon that made her look even more elegant. "Alexandra, you make a beautiful bride."

"Love makes any woman beautiful—isn't that what they say?" Alexandra did feel like a princess in her gown of white silk. The wedding ring sparkled on her left hand. A beautiful ring. "I never should have let you do most of the cooking and baking for the buffet, but it's a great success. Thank you."

"Oh, my pleasure, my dear. Goodness." Bev wrapped her in a warm embrace, loving and motherly. ''To think you're my daughter now. What fun we'll have. I told John he can't keep you away too long on that mysterious honeymoon he's got planned.''

''Trying to find out where he's taking me, are you?'' Alexandra was brimming with the secret. John was taking her through the national parks of the West on a luxurious driving tour. He'd bought a new car for the occasion. They were taking Hailey, too. Alexandra's first real family vacation, and they were going to do it right.

Joy filled her heart, filled her soul.

''Here's a little surprise from me.'' Bev pressed something into Alexandra's hand. ''Welcome to our family, sweetheart. Oh, there's Helen. I must speak with her.''

As Bev hurried away, Alexandra looked at the bundle in her hand. A stack of handwritten cards tied in a pretty yellow ribbon. ''A few of my treasured recipes, since you are now a cherished member of the family. Love always, Bev.''

''Hey, it's not right for a bride to be alone.'' John's voice, John's touch. His tender kiss on her cheek. ''What are you thinking? That you should've run for the hills while you had a chance?''

''Yep. Too bad I forgot my tennis shoes. I can't get far in these heels.'' She leaned into his welcoming arms, savored his strong embrace. "I love you, John."

"I love you." His hand cupped her nape, tenderly. "It's a beautiful day, don't you think?"

"Yes. It's going to be a beautiful life."

The past had faded away, Patrick was in jail, and she'd found a place to belong. Her Bible Study friends waved to her from the table on the back lawn. A few women from the choir were accompanying the church's pianist as she coaxed "Amazing Grace" from the keyboard. Hailey in her lilac maid-of-honor dress raced through the backyard with best friends Stephanie and Christa, while Angel followed, barking with delight.

Alexandra felt whole. God was truly good, for showering her with these precious blessings. And the best one of all took her hand in his and leaned close to whisper in her ear, "You have tears in your eyes. Happy ones? Or sad ones?"

"John." She leaned her cheek on his chest, settling into his arms, where she was meant to be. "I'm happy."

"Good, my love. Because this is just the start of our good life together." The proof of it was in his kiss, in his tenderness and in the brush of their souls. It left no doubt. Theirs was a true love, blessed from above, a bright glowing light that would forever burn.

* * * * *

Dear Reader,

Thank you so much for choosing *Heaven Knows*.
While I was writing Alexandra and John's story, I
began with the idea of a woman on the run looking for
safety and ended up with something more. This is the
story of a woman who has never known real love and
finds it in the arms of a strong and tender man.

Love is one of the Lord's greatest gifts to us, and one
of the most powerful forces in the universe. Whether in
romance novels or in real life, love does triumph over
all.

Wishing you love and peace,

Jillian Hart

THE CARPENTER'S WIFE

BY

LENORA WORTH

No one wanted roots more than Rock Dempsey.
He finally met the woman he wanted to share his life
with in Ana Hanson. But nothing had ever come easy
for the woman he hoped to have and to hold forever.
Would it take some divine guidance from above
before she would become the carpenter's wife?

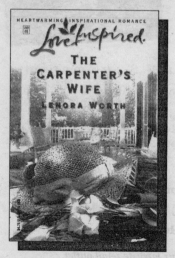

Don't miss
THE CARPENTER'S WIFE
On sale June 2003

*Available at your
favorite retail outlet.*

TOWARD HOME

BY

CAROLYNE AARSEN

All her life, Melanie Visser yearned for the stately, gingerbread Victorian in the town where she grew up. Moving back home, she discovers her dream house is for sale. And though the long-neglected manor needs some tender loving care, its embittered owner needs God's healing touch—and Melanie's sweet kindness—even more.

Don't miss

TOWARD HOME

On sale July 2003

Available at your favorite retail outlet.

Visit us at www.steeplehill.com

LITH